THE BALLAD OF BIG BEN'S BOOTS

AND OTHER TALES FOR TELLING

To Kitty: Best wishes,

THE BALLAD OF BIG BEN'S BOOTS
AND OTHER TALES FOR TELLING

BY
JOHN DASHNEY

John Dashney

ILLUSTRATED BY SHEILA SOMERVILLE

1999
4

SEATTLE, WASHINGTON

1996

STORM PEAK PRESS

157 YESLER WAY, SUITE 413

SEATTLE, WASHINGTON 98104

© 1994, JOHN DASHNEY
ISBN 0-9641357-3-6
LIBRARY OF CONGRESS CATALOG CARD NUMBER: 96-67227

© 1996, JOHN DASHNEY
SECOND EDITION 1996

*This book is for grandfathers in general
and two in particular:*

H. L. Braden & Jack Dashney

Where would I have been without you?

CONTENTS

Introduction: The Stage Within Your Mind

Let's take a stroll behind your eyes
And see what we can find,
As we explore the setting for
The stage within your mind.

A few words about these stories. . . .

I began telling tales in the 1970's because I had no choice. My son liked to hear stories, but I was losing my sight and could no longer read to him.

It is impossible to hold a large children's book with one hand, a big reading lens with another, and a wriggling three- or four-year-old with yet another. I attempted it. You run out of hands.

So I tried faking it by putting down the lens, trying to remember the story as best I could, and turning a page every now and then to make it look good. But my son was a very smart boy and soon figured that one out, especially after the time he caught me holding the book upside down and *reading* it back to front.

"Daddy!" he scolded. "You're not reading that story! You're *telling* it!"

"Yep," I admitted.

"That's all right," he said. "I like it better that way anyhow."

So I stopped pretending and threw the book away; been doing it that way ever since.

First, I tried doing traditional stories or ones I had read somewhere. One day, while I was trying to remember and tell a rather dull and boring story, a very interesting thought suddenly hit me: I can write better than that!

So I did. Or at least, I tried.

There were several to share with my son. When he started school, there were a few more to share with his class. Then came the other first grade room. Then the second grade down the hall, and then the third and the fourth. . . .

Before I realized, I was loaned out to another school. One of my son's teachers had a friend who taught elsewhere. And this friend had another friend who taught at a third school, who had yet another friend who taught at a fourth. . . . Well, you get the idea.

Eventually, one of the teachers said to me, "You know, you really ought to get paid for this." So the necessity turned into a hobby, and the hobby turned into a business.

Now, almost twenty years later, my once-little boy is quite a bit bigger than I am, and I have spun my tales in more than five hundred schools on four continents.

And I am writing this book. Why?

There have been other books. *The Adventures of Walter the Weremouse* and its sequel, *The Adventures of Mishka the Mousewere*, developed from a story that got way too long to tell. Most of these stories are ones I have told to thousands of children (and adults). Many more haven't been and won't be, because I can't go everywhere. So I hope this book will introduce my tales to a still larger audience.

Some of them are not in my telling collection. "The Bear Hunters" was written for a special anthology of stories about teddy bears, though the editor never brought the book out. Finally it gets into print here. "The Plain Princess" never got long enough to be a full-length book, but it did get too long to tell in one sitting. I still like it though, and here is a chance to share it with others.

"Mr. Skink & Mr. Skunk" and "The Fox and the Squirrel" are new stories added for this edition. They are now in my telling collection.

"The Great Chicken Stampede" is also in this collection, told by Wilbur the Wrangler. Wilbur is a little fella, just six inches tall, who worked in the old days for Colonel Sanders on his huge chicken ranch. He, who rode a big white Canada goose named Honky, and his friend Max, whose trusty steed was a dachshund named Fritz, were the heroes of several stories that my son and I developed. There were too many to include all in this book, and not enough to make a book by themselves. So I chose this one as a fair sample. Wilbur is a good yarnspinner, so I'll let him tell his own story.

Also included is "Sam Samson's Simulated Sheep." No fair just reading this one silently. This is a tongue-twister, even though it does have a plot, sort of. See if you can get to where you say it in under seven minutes with three or fewer mistakes. Good luck!

Now, I have a question for you.

Where are you right now as you read this? Perhaps in a bookstore? Maybe curled up in a quiet corner of the library? Or snug in your own room? These are okay places for introductions, but not for stories that are meant to be shared.

Gather yourself an audience; maybe a pretend audience while you practice. Pretend audiences are great. They always laugh or cheer or sigh at all the right places and applaud loudly at the end. Work with them first. Then, when you think you are ready, you can try with a real audience.

After all, these stories were written to be heard and meant to be performed. And what good is performing if there is no one around to hear or watch?

Remember too, these stories were written on paper and not chiseled in rock. If you want to change one and do it differently, go right ahead! For all stories. . . .

Enough of this! Introductions are supposed to be short. So read on! Enjoy! And share!

For who knows where the tale may lead
Or how the plot may wind
Among the twists and turnings on
The stage within your mind?

– John Dashney

Mr. Skink and Mr. Skunk

Mr. Skink and Mr. Skunk
Kept a shop that was full of junk.
What kind of junk? — you might just think —
Some broken pens and dried-up ink,
(Contributed by Mr. Skink)
And a big old trunk of gooey gunk
That Mr. Skunk sold by the hunk.

But not a soul came in to buy,
And can you guess the reason why?
Well, who would ever want to try
A slab of year-old apple pie?
Or a needle made without an eye?
Mr. Skink said, "My, oh my!"
While Mr. Skunk began to sigh.

"I think we're sunk!" cried Mr. Skunk.
"No one comes to buy our junk!
What do you think, my good friend Skink?"
And Mr. Skink then poured a drink
And gave his good friend Skunk a wink,
And said, "I'll tell you what I think.
Our profits have begun to shrink.

So I think we should have a sale,
And sell our junk off by the pail.
With such a sale, we cannot fail
To push our profits off the scale.
We'll send out coupons through the mail
And put up signs along the trail.
I'll hammer. You can hold the nail!"

"Oh no, Friend Skink!" said Mr. Skunk.
"Although I want to sell our junk,

It seems too risky — so I think —
To let an old nearsighted skink,
Who really is quite on the brink
Of blindness, hammer with a clunk
Upon this poor unlucky skunk!"

Then Mr. Skink, who had been sad,
Quite suddenly got very mad
And muttered to himself, "Egad!
This Skunk is really quite a cad
To say my sight is going bad!"
(Though just that afternoon he had
Mistook Skunk for his dear old dad.)

"I think you stink!" yelled Mr. Skink,
"That's bunk! You're drunk!" cried Mr. Skunk,
Who stepped behind a pile of junk
And threw a chunk of gooey gunk
That hit *ker-plink!* on Mr. Skink.
Skink threw it back; it went *ker-plunk!*
Upon the head of Mr. Skunk.

So Skink and Skunk got in a fight
That lasted almost all the night.
All their neighbors soon took fright
And hid themselves until daylight,
Because it was an awful sight

To see the way that Skink would bite,
While Skunk sprayed Skink with all his might.

"I'm in a funk!" cried Mr. Skunk.
"This fight has ruined all our junk!"
"I'm tickled pink!" said Mr. Skink,
"To go my way and break our link.
Let each of us now swim or sink!"
And off then Mr. Skink did slink,
Right after Mr. Skunk had slunk.

And when the sun came up next day,
Both Skink and Skunk were far away.
All the neighbors cried, "Hooray!"
And had themselves a holiday.
And to this day (or so they say)
They meet to celebrate and play.
And when they do, they always say:

"Never shall we buy our junk
From Mr. Skink or Mr. Skunk!"

Edwin the Elephant

A strange thing occurred last week at the zoo.
You may not believe it, but I'm sure it was true.
The day was quite warm, with scarcely a breeze,
When Edwin the Elephant couldn't quite. . . sneeze!

Now, he could say, "Aah!" But he couldn't say, "Choo!"
No! That part was stuck, and it couldn't get through
His bodacious long trunk which hung clear to the ground.
It stuck there pulsating, and spun round and round,
And tormented and tortured and tickled poor Ed,
Till he moaned and he groaned and then finally said,
"Won't somebody help me? Won't somebody please
Tell me how to get rid of a not-quite-yet sneeze?"

Armaund the Aardvark then spoke up and said,
"Wheenevair I get ze sneeze stuck in *my* head,
Zen I burrow my way down deep in ze ground,
I eat bugs and worms, all juicy and round!
Zen, if I find zat I still cannot sneeze,
I chew on ze roots of ze foozle-nut trees!
For zere taste is so vile zat you'll sneeze out your brains!
And zen keep on sneezing till nothing remains!
So if you have ze sneeze zat you cannot get out,
I suggest zat you grub in ze dirt with your snout!"

5

"No thank you!" cried Edwin. "I'd rather not grub!
For I don't want my trunk to be worn to a nub!
And as for chewing on roots of foozle-nut trees,
Why, I'd rather swallow a gallon of fleas,
Or a stack of old leaves!
Or anything else that would make me sneeze!
There's Seigfried the Seal! Could you tell me, please,
Just how to get rid of my not-quite-yet sneeze?"

"Ach himmel!" cried Seigfried. "Has dis ellerfunken
Got der sneezle und wheezle all stuck mit der trunken?
Und der Ah! und der Choo! all mixed up togedder?
Den ve tickle his nose mit ein gross ostrick fedder!
For to work der schnozz daily, mit bustles und hustles,
Is ein grand thing for building der grossen sneeze muscles!
Und den, when der sneeze is *alles kaput*,
You can balance a ball on der end of der snoot!
Und when you can juggle der cup und der dish,
Der keeper will give you a meal. . . of raw fish!"

To which Edwin said, "Yuck! I'd rather have hay!
Or peanuts or elephant food any day!
But I can't while I've got this old not-quite-yet sneeze!
Won't somebody, somebody, *somebody* please
Tell me how to get rid of my not-quite-yet sneeze?
I've asked a French aardvark, and a German seal too,

And all of the things that they told me to do
Were things that no elephant ever would try,
But if I don't sneeze, I'm afraid I will die!
Would Paddy O'Panda be able to ease
The itch and the twitch of a not-quite-yet sneeze?"

"Ah, faith now!" said Paddy. "There's no trouble to that!
I can give you the answer in five seconds flat!
Just lay on your back, with your paws in the air,
Then curl up in a ball and the sneeze will be there!"

"Don't you think," Edwin said, "it would look a bit strange
For an *elephant* to lay on his back and arrange
His legs and his trunk all up in the air?
I'm quite sure that people would snicker and stare!"

"Then why not just hop on the zookeeper's lap,
And cuddle and snuggle and take a short nap?
For that's what I do when things bother me,
It's an answer as simple as simple can be!"

"If an *elephant* hopped on the zookeeper's lap,"
Said Edwin, "he'd *squash* him, as flat as a map
Of the far-away flatlands of Flanders or France!
No, I don't think I'll hop till the Saturday dance!
But isn't there somebody, *somebody* please,
Who could help me get rid of my not-quite-yet sneeze?"

"Perhaps I could help you," said Mortimer Mouse,
As he crawled out from under the elephant's house.
"For I'm small, and I see things that others cannot.
Perhaps there is something that, well, you forgot."
"I doubt it," said Edwin, "but give it a try,
For if I don't sneeze, I am sure I will die!"

So Mortimer crawled into Edwin's long trunk
And, "Aha!" he cried, "I think, thank and thunk
I've discovered the reason why you cannot sneeze.
Your trunk is stopped up, just as tight as you please!
Why, it looks like the plug from your *bathtub* is there!
I could pull it out, but — oh my! — do I dare?
Because right behind it is a horrible choo!"
But Edwin begged, "Pull it! Oh, pull it! Please do!"

So Mortimer Mouse grabbed a'hold of the plug,
And he gave it a tug, and a tug, and a *tug!*
Till out came the plug with a "Pop!" It is true!
And right close behind it came Edwin's big "Choooo!"

Then people and critters for ten miles around
All pondered and wondered, "Just what was that sound?"
"It sounded like thunder; we'd better go back!"
"No! It was a cannon; we're under attack!"
But it was just Edwin, who finally sneezed!
And now that it's over, he feels mighty pleased.

And so ends our story, except one more bit:
He blasted poor Mortimer Mouse. . . into orbit!
And as Edwin now sniffs at the trees and the flowers,
Mortimer flies over every two hours,
Becoming the very first mouse astronaut;
I'd tell even more lines, except. . . I forgot!

The Orm:
A Christmas Story

On the day before Christmas at the icy North Pole,
When Santa is checking his big master roll
Of the millions of girls and the millions of boys
Who were good enough to receive Christmas toys.
And the elves are washing and waxing the sleigh
And feeding the reindeer their oats and their hay,
And old Mrs. Claus is packing some fruit
In the pocket of Santa's red traveling suit.

As an elf cleans the harness and another one sews,
And new batteries are tested in Rudolph's red nose.
When the takeoff lights blink through the Christmas Eve snow,
And the flight plan computer says, "All systems go!"
There's still one more thing for old Santa to do
Before preparations for takeoff are through.
Make sure that the sleigh is packed full and warm.
"And, yes," says Santa, "let's get out the orm!"

"Now just what's an orm?" I hear everyone say.
Well, it's a creature that isn't around much today.
In fact, there's just one that we know of, I fear,

And he works for old Santa one night every year.
He's fifty feet long, and about one foot wide,
With billions of bristles all over his hide.
He doesn't have fingers. He doesn't have toes.
And no arms or legs, 'far as anyone knows.
He just crawls like a snake, has a head like a knob,
And he works for old Santa, and this is his job.

Have you ever wondered how Santa keeps clean,
With all of those grimy, black chimneys? I mean,
Millions of chimneys from Utah to Maine!
From the snowy Dakotas to the cold Texas plain!
And that's just America, think of the mess!
Think of the squiggling and think of the stress!
If the fire's still burning; that's always the worst!
'Course, the answer to that is: the orm goes down first!

He first checks for smoke and then puts out the fire,
Then with each old bristle as tough as a wire,
The chimney is scrubbed clean of ashes and soot.
Then back up he goes, inch by inch, foot by foot,
Till the chimney is ready for Santa to use
With never a scrape and never a bruise.

And while Saint Nick is filling the stockings below,
The orm cleans himself with a roll in the snow

Or the grass or the mud if it's raining that night.
Then Saint Nick whistles softly, and quick as a light,
The orm scrambles back up — or so I am told —
Drops his tail down the chimney and Saint Nick grabs hold.
Then Santa whispers, "All clear! Haul away!"
And the orm hauls him up! Santa hops in his sleigh.
While the orm curls himself round the runners to dry,
Saint Nick cracks his whip, and off they both fly!

By the time the night's over, is there any doubt
That the orm and old Santa are both quite worn out?
They fly back up north as the dawn streaks the sky
And land at the Pole with a groan and a sigh.
Then the elves all come running, the reindeer get fed,
Santa has a hot toddy, then goes straight to bed.
And the orm is unwound from the back of the sleigh
And washed by ten elves, who work night and day
For more than a week just to get out the ashes
And soot from his bristles and scales and eyelashes.
Then he's fed a big dinner (or so I believe)
And curls up to sleep until next Christmas Eve.

And Santa is happy throughout the whole year.
He knows with the orm he has nothing to fear.
"I'll be ready for Christmas," he says. "Don't you worry.
I won't have to fret and I won't have to hurry.

For while the orm's with me, I'll always stay clean
And dash up the chimney; after all, I'm not lean!
I'll fly through the night. I'll fly through the storm.
But I'll not fly anywhere without my dear orm!"

The Awful Waffle

Now, one mornin' Grandpappy jumped outa bed,
Pulled his britches on over his head,
Turned to Grandma, who was sleeping, and said,

"Don't bother gettin' up early this mornin', Old Woman,
'cause I'm gonna fix breakfast myself!"

She didn't hear him, and that was too bad, 'cause she'd
have put a stop to that nonsense mighty quick!

So Grandpappy hurried on down to the kitchen,
With his eyes all aglow and his mustache a-twitchin',
And he says to himself, "By George, I'm a'itchin'
To fix me a waffle, yessir!

I don't know quite how it's done, but it can't be too
hard. I'll just use what's logical and likely and easy to
come by!"

So he mixed some flour and milk in a pan,
Tossed in some eggs and a handful of bran,
And then stirred it all up, that silly old man!
But it still didn't look right, nosir!

"Maybe I shoulda broken the eggs *before* I put 'em in,"
he thought. "It sure doesn't hold together very well. I'll
add in a little glue to give it some consistency! And the
white stuff in this here box; it *looks* a lot like flour, even
though the box says, uh, l-a-u-n-d-r-y d-e-t-e-r-g-e-n-t?
Well, we'll try some of that too! *Now* we're cookin'!"

Then he poured it on a waffle iron to see how it would bake,
And he hoped that it would turn out light
    and fluffy like a cake.
But it didn't take him long to see; he'd made a bad mistake!
And he'd cooked up the world's most awful. . . waffle!

I mean, that there waffle just jumped right up off the
waffle iron, spun around on the counter three or four
times, looked up at Grandpappy and said, "You just try
to eat me, Old Man! I double-dog dare you!"

"No thankee!" Grandpa said, and he said it mighty quick.
"You just get on out a'fore I beat you with a stick!
Or maybe throw you in the fire or toss you in the crick.
But one thing's for certain sure!
I ain't gonna take a jawful off such an awful. . . waffle!"

So he beat that waffle with his hands
    and kicked it with his feet
Until it flew right out the door and rolled on down the street.
And who do you think it happened to meet?

15

Why a totally zonked-out skateboarder, who said, "Ooooh woooow, Man! A Frisbee! Kinda funny-lookin' one, but I'll give it a toss. Oooooh woooow, Dude! There it gooooooes!"

Now, I don't know just who was to blame.
Maybe that thrower didn't know how to aim.
But whatever the reason, all the witnesses claim:

That awful waffle flew right through the open window of a house, bounced twice on a polyester rug, and hit a nearsighted computer programmer right in the leg! And he thought, "It must be some new kind of ultra high-density computer disk! I'll put it in my brand-new CPU and see how it computes!"

So he shoved it in his CPU and started pushing keys,
And the computer gave a kinda cough,
and then a kinda wheeze.
And finally, with a well-programmed and scientific sneeze,

It shot that awful waffle right back out through the window, across the street and into another house, where someone else thought it must be some brand-new kind of old-fashioned record album, and stuck it on an old but still-working stereo player!

16

Now, have you ever heard a waffle being played on a stereo?

The music that it makes really isn't very merry-o.

In fact, I can say without bein' too contrary-o,

It sounded just about like sixty-seven fingernails being scraped down a chalkboard all at the same time! Sorta made your teeth crawl, and your hair grate and your skin stand on end.

And then a silly lady tried to wear it for a hat!

And when that didn't work, she tried to feed it to her cat!

But the kitty went, "Meeooww!" and arched its back
and hissed and spat!

It wouldn't even try a jawful of such an awful. . . waffle!

So a big policeman, with his siren a-blowin'

Took the waffle back to Grandpappy and said, "You're goin'

To keep this waffle chained and locked,
'cause you should be a'knowin',

It is absolutely unlawful to cook up such an awful. . . waffle!

And so that waffle still remains on Grandpa's closet shelf.

And as for any other verses, well, make 'em up yourself.

But even if you were a troll, a gremlin or an elf,

Would you be mean enough to fill yer maw and paw full

Of such an awful. . . waffle? Well, I hope not!

Old Mr. Suggs

Old Mr. Suggs kept a house full of bugs,
Because he preferred them to people.
He didn't like rats and he didn't like cats,
Nor the bats that lived in the steeple.

So he kept as a dweller, way down in the cellar,
A most disagreeable hornet.
He would give it citations for sting violations,
And with ribbons and medals adorn it.

And wasps by the dozens (I think they were cousins.)
Flew out on patrol every night,
Stinging salesmen, and teachers and visiting preachers,
And gave politicians a fright.

A great big tarantula he'd nicknamed Gargantua
Had been trained to answer the door.
But the callers all ran, every woman and man,
And they never came back any more!

A devout praying mantis who came from Atlantis
Preached to bugs of all denominations.
His sermons had power, but then he'd devour
About half of all his congregations.

Some red and some black ants, in form-fitting sweatpants,
Played volleyball with a green pea.
They had two big roaches to serve as their coaches,
And a dung beetle as referee.

The silkworms kept busy — some even got dizzy —
In spinning out silk for Suggs' clothes.
While the spiders wove frames for fantastic games
Of tic tac that he played with his toes.

There were several old moths that Suggs used for cloths
To wipe dishes and spills from the floor.

But since they didn't last and ran out rather fast,
He kept six hundred more in a drawer.

A butterfly fluttered by out of the sky:
A beautiful sight, I am certain.
So in the cold weather, Suggs glued thousands together,
And hung them up as his living room curtain.

But my question to you is just what can you do
With the lowly and poor caterpillar?
Well, when there was need, it was certain, indeed,
That Old Suggs would know how to fill 'er.

You see, these woolly bugs Suggs wove into rugs;
He laid them out on his floor.
Each room was improved, and when Suggs moved,
His rugs followed him right out the door.

Suggs kept his house bright throughout the long night,
And instead of electricity, he'd use
Six pounds of lightning bugs, penned in old cider jugs,
And they never once blew a fuse.

Two thousand bedbugs, very strong and well-fed bugs,
Massaged Suggs to sleep every night.
While one hundred crickets from out of the thickets
Chirped lullabies; what a delight!

And right by his head, when Suggs went to bed,
Sat a bottle of glowworms all night.
For the bedroom was gloomy and a little too roomy,
But with a nightlight, Suggs always slept tight.

In all of the land there was no marching band
Like the centipedes Old Suggs had trained.
Each with a hundred feet always keeping up the beat,
And the rhythm and cadence maintained

By swarms of mosquitoes who nibbled on Fritos
As they rode on the centipedes' backs.
They droned and they hummed
  till your senses were numbed,
And they left teeny crumbs in their tracks.

And so ends my story and all of its gory
Description — I hope it will stick —
About Old Mr. Suggs and his house full of bugs.
I think I'm going to be sick!

The Runaway Tree

Once upon a time there was a tree that lived on a lawn, close by a house, in a town somewhere. For many years a big family had lived in this house. Each year the father raked up the tree's leaves as they fell to the ground. The mother gathered in its fruit, and the children climbed it and built forts and treehouses in its branches.

But the children grew up and moved away. The mother and father grew old and sold the house, and they too moved away. And the new owner was a lazy man, who let the leaves lie and the fruit spoil on the ground.

One day the tree heard him say to his wife, "I'm tired of that stupid old tree. I think I'll hire a man to cut it down and saw it up into firewood!"

Well, as you can imagine, the tree was not happy with *that* piece of news. "Me? Cut down?" it said to itself. "Right in my prime? To be burned in a fireplace just so that lazy slob can warm his smelly feet? Hey! I'm not gonna stick around for that! I'm gonna go where I can get me some respect!"

So, late that night, the tree pulled up its roots, one after another, and tiptoed — or perhaps we should say, tip-rooted — across the street, where it pushed and it shoved and it wriggled and squirmed until — *shoonk!* — it planted itself on another lawn!

But when the tree's new owner looked out his kitchen window the next morning, he dropped his cup of coffee right into his scrambled eggs and cried out, "Great

Lord o' Mercy, Elizabeth! There's a great big tree a-growin' out on our front yard!"

"Great big trees don't suddenly appear, George! Have you been sippin' at the sauce again?"

But just at that moment the lazy man from across the street came banging on their front door. "How dare you steal my tree!" he shouted. "My beautiful tree! My wonderful tree! I'm gonna have you arrested!"

"What do you mean, steal your tree?" George replied. "How dare you plant your mangy old tree on my beautiful lawn? I'm gonna sue you for everything you've got!"

"I'll have you arrested!"

"I'll take you to court!"

"Robber!"

"Sneak!"

"Treenapper!"

"Treedumper!"

And so they shouted back and forth all day, while the tree shook its branches in disgust.

"Well!" it said to itself. "If they're gonna act like that, then I'm just gonna go someplace else!"

So, late that night, the tree pulled up its roots once again and tiprooted off down the street, looking for a place where it could find some respect. The pavement was very hard on its poor roots, which weren't used to this sort of traveling, after all; and it had an *awful* time ducking under power lines.

And before it had gone three blocks, a big policeman pulled it over and gave it a ticket! For tiprooting the wrong way up a one-way street, making an improper left turn, tiprooting through a red light, failing to yield the right-of-way to an oncoming rosebush and using the public streets and highways without having the proper license plates!

"Wow!" said the tree to itself. "It's gonna take a whole year's worth of fruit just to pay for these tickets! I sure can't get any respect around here. I know! They say that trees on golf courses get lots of respect. That's where I'll go!"

So the runaway tree tiprooted all the way out to the golf course, where it attempted to join a grove of trees that stretched along one of the fairways. But these golf course trees were terrible snobs! They looked down their branches at this newcomer, and rustled their bark and shook their leaves and said:

"*We* are specially bred and manicured trees, who have been put here especially to make this place look beautiful. *You* are nothing more than a common lawn tree. Why, it's obvious that no one has pruned you for years! You're still wearing some of last season's leaves! You may even have: *bugs!* Get out! Get out! You don't belong here with us!"

The poor runaway tree felt terribly sad. Nobody wanted it! It was so tired, and its roots were so sore! So it tiprooted out into the middle of the fairway, where it pushed and it shoved and it wriggled and squirmed until — *shoonk!* — it planted itself in the soft, cool earth beneath the green grass.

"You'll be sorry!" the other trees warned. "Just you wait!"

And the runaway tree did wait, until morning, when a big golf tournament started up! Two hundred and sixty-two golfers began hitting shots right down the fairway, straight at the runaway tree! "Ouchie! Oochie! Ohoho my golly!" cried the poor tree to itself as golf balls whizzed through its branches or got tangled in its leaves or bounced off its trunk.

"Feldenblatz and blasted cinnabarbsen!" cried the golfers (along with worse things that can't be printed here) as they saw their best shots go ricocheting off in all directions, and they all had to take double and triple bogies on the hole. "Who put that stupid tree in the middle of the fairway? It's not fair! It's not right! We'll never play this course again!"

"Don't worry," said the course manager. "We'll cut it down first thing tomorrow."

"Oh no!" said the poor tree to itself. "I have to move again tonight! But I'm so tired! And my roots are so sore! And nobody — *nobody* — wants me! I think I'll just go down to the river and throw myself in and float down to the ocean and become driftwood! Maybe some of the trees along the riverbank will have a friendly word for me as I go by."

So, late that night, the poor tree pulled up its roots once again and tiprooted down to the river. But when it reached the riverbank, there were no other trees to be seen, just some scrubby little bushes.

"What has happened here?" it asked a bush. "Where are all the trees that should be here?"

"A big fire came through here last year and burned everything right down to the river," the bush answered. "We're all that's been able to grow back."

"Are there no little trees?" asked the runaway tree. "Are there no seedlings?"

"None!" said the bush. "It's so lonesome here without any trees! Would you stay and live with us, please?"

And when it heard that, the runaway tree forgot all about falling into the river. Slowly, painfully, but for the last time, it pushed and it shoved and it wriggled and squirmed until — shoonk! — it planted itself in the soft, wet earth next to the river!

The very next morning, two birds landed in its branches and began building a nest. Then some squirrels found a hollow place in its trunk and turned it into their den.

"Plant some of my fruit in the soil along the river!" it begged the birds and squirrels, and they did. And soon little seedlings began to sprout.

The old tree looked up at the sun and the sky and waved its branches in thanks, because at last it was where it wanted to be. And at last it had found some respect.

26

Ishmael the Clam

Way down on the shoreline of the Bay of Hazaam,
At the edge of a tidepool lived Ishmael the Clam.
He lived with six brothers, and six hundred aunts,
And five hundred uncles, plus all his pet plants.
And twenty-two sisters, one mom and one dad,
And ten thousand cousins (some good and some bad)!
They lived in the clam beds, just as happy as. . . clams.
And they dined every day on fresh barnacle hams.
Their lives were quite pleasant, except for one thing:
This Ishmael the Clam loved to howl, scream and sing!

Well now, who ever heard of a musical clam?
Not once in the history of the Bay of Hazaam
Had those thousands of clams even made a small chirp!
No! They thought it was rude to hiccup or burp!
Or caw like the seagulls or croak like the frogs;
Clams just spoke in whispers or were silent as pogs!
And they whispered so softly from deep in the shell
That you never could hear all the secrets they'd tell.
So imagine their shock on a night late in June
When Ishmael quite suddenly. . . howled at the moon!

Egad! What a noise! All through the tide pools
Clams opened their shells and then gaped like dumb fools!
"Who's making that racket? It's a sin! It's a crime!"
"Our bay has been silent for such a long time!"
"Now the seagulls are shocked and the barnacles flustered!"
"The lobsters all blush, and the water's like mustard!"
And just who could be making this terrible noise?
Why, it couldn't be one of the clam girls or boys!
But it was! It was Ishmael who howled at the moon
By the Bay of Hazaam on a night late in June.

And just how could this clam shout and holler so well?
Ah! The secret lay in his amplified shell
That could pick up the radio or the TV,
From the six o'clock news on Channel 3
To the Top 40 hits on a disc jockey's show.
He could sing like a rock group or caw like a crow,
Make a noise like a gun or a runaway train,
Or an audience laughing; in fact, it was plain
That there wasn't a louder, more talented clam
In the pools by the edge of the Bay of Hazaam!

So the clams held a meeting to decide what to do,
And one old clam whispered, "What's this bay coming to?
When young whippersnappers can holler like brats!
He ought to be muzzled; and that, Sirs, is thats!"

Then the President whispered for order and stated,
"This continual noise cannot be tolerated!
So Ishmael, you must stop this horrible racket
Or we'll hand you your suitcase and tell you to pack it,
And send you away as a poor exiled clam,
Far, far away from the Bay of Hazaam!"

What a terrible choice! If he chose to obey,
And shut his shell tightly, why, then he could stay.
But Ish loved to sing and to howl at the moon,
(Which was big, round and full on that night late in June)
And then hear his echo bounce through the tide pools;
It was grand, it was fun, but against all the rules
That govern each small individual clam
In the pools by the edge of the Bay of Hazaam.

So Ishmael decided. This clam chose. . . to go!
And the same old clam then whispered, "I told you so!
I know what happens to a clam who gets snippy,
And who leaves his fine home to live like a hippie.
He'll go off by himself and howl all the louder,
And get caught by a digger and put in a chowder!
So just you remember and don't be surprised,
When you hear that this Ishmael has been chowderized!
And becomes the main course at a digger festivity,
For ignoring our rules on un-clamlike activity!

It may serve as a warning to other young clam,
Not to leave a fine home on the Bay of Hazaam!"

Ish's mom packed his suitcase and made him a lunch
Of plankton and barnacle hams he could munch.
"Now Ishmael, remember to write us," she said.
"But don't call! Clams only whisper in our tidepool bed."
Ish picked up his suitcase, then said, "So long!"
And went his own way, while humming a song.
But clams move so slowly, in squibbles and squinches,
That it took quite awhile just to cover six inches.
In fact, it might take forty years for this clam
To hike all the way 'cross the Bay of Hazaam.

But Ish was determined to do his own thing.
He wanted to warble and yodel and sing,
And make many noises not befitting a clam
Who comes from the calm, peaceful Bay of Hazaam.
So his friends said goodbye as he crawled slowly past,
And all of his cousins, from the first to the last,
Both the good and the bad and the young and the old,
Gave him advice how not to catch a cold.
(Or the flu or such ailments that bother a clam
Who runs off from calm, peaceful Bay of Hazaam.)

Now the bright morning sun found this clam far away.
Ish had squirmed and he'd squinched thirty feet 'cross the bay!
(A distance in clam terms that truly was frightful!)
But Ishmael just thought it was all quite delightful
To be free from the rules that governed each clam
In the pools by the edge of the Bay of Hazaam.
So he stopped and he howled,
   though the moon had gone down.
But instead of an echo, poor Ish heard a sound
That would raise every hair on a poor frightened clam:
The starfish were coming to the Bay of Hazaam!

A whole army of starfish came marching along!
There were line after line of them, six thousand strong!
They were led by their king, old Six-Finger Grizzle;
Just the sound of his name made a clam's temper sizzle!
They were hungry and mean, and they wanted to feast
On those poor little clams! Every mean starfish beast
Had been drooling and smacking chops with delight!
(Slurp! Slurp! Slurp! Sluuurp!)
"We'll ambush them clams, and before they can fight,
We will guzzle them all — to the very last clam —
In those pools by the edge of the Bay of Hazaam!"

But the starfish did not know that Ishmael was near,
And that he overheard them, for starfish can't hear

As well as a clam, who is used to a whisper.
No, a starfish roars loudly, for he's deaf as a blister.
Which is why they passed by with just inches to spare,
Not noticing Ishmael the clam hiding there;
So intent were they all on their upcoming dinner,
Instead of Ishmael contemplating, "To clams I'm a sinner.
Yet my duty's to warn every large and small clam
In the pools by the edge of the Bay of Hazaam!"

So he opened his shell, and he let out a yell
That was heard in the beds just as clear as a bell.
"The starfish are coming! Protect yourselves, brothers!
Protect all your sisters and cousins and mothers!"
And then just to make sure his warning was heard,
He mimicked the cry of a cockatoo bird!
Then he roared like a lion and croaked like a frog,
And next did the howl of an old hunting dog!
Never ever before had just one single clam
Made such noise in the pools of the Bay of Hazaam!

When the clams heard his warning, they got set for battle!
They sharpened their shells, and the loud, angry rattle
Of those thousands of clam shells, all ready to snip,
And to pinch, and to bite, and to grab, and to nip,
Made the bay waters churn and the fish gasp with fear,
As the army of starfish drew near; they were here!

But imagine the shock that those mean starfish had,
When they found that their dinner was waiting and mad!
And snipping for battle! thanks to Ishmael the Clam,
Who had warned all the rest on the Bay of Hazaam!

Old Six-Finger Grizzle went purple with rage,
And bellowed, "Attack!" which was just not a sage
Or a good or a smart or a wise thing to do.
"We'll have them for dinner before we are through!"
But when clams have been warned and are ready to fight,
They can be mighty mean when they pinch, nip and bite!
When the starfish attacked, they found out it was true,
That an old angry clam can nip noses in two!
And that starfish lose toes when they mess with a clam
From the pools by the edge of the Bay of Hazaam!

So snap-snappity-snap! and snip-snippity snip!
All the clams gave those starfish a bite and a nip!
They sent them off howling with bites on the noses
And pinches and scratches and a few missing toeses!
And just which of the starfish ran fastest that day?
Why, old Six-Finger Grizzle, their king, so they say!
He was way out in front, and he thought he was free,
But there was one clam that he just didn't see.
It was Ishmael, the bravest and loneliest clam
Of the thousands who lived in the Bay of Hazaam!

Little Ish saw him coming, and he knew they would meet.
So he reached out and nipped one of Grizzle's big feet!
His sharp shell clamped down, and the old starfish yelled.
But Ishmael held on, and he held and he held!
Grizzle kicked and he pinched and he fought and he bit,
But Ishmael kept holding, even though he got hit!
Till Grizzle was glad just to get out alive;
But instead of six fingers, now he only had five!
He left one in the jaws of the brave little clam
Who had saved all the rest on the Bay of Hazaam!

So Ishmael came home, and they welcomed him back.
They unpacked his suitcase and made him a snack
Of plankton and barnacle hams he could munch.
For fighting the battle had made him miss lunch!
Then they made him the Watch Clam, and now every day
Through the pools at the edge of that bright little bay,
You can hear our friend Ish, as he cries every hour,
At the top of his voice and with all of his power,
"All is well! I'm alert to protect every clam
In the pools by the edge of the Bay of Hazaam!"

If You Can Carry the Cat

In a long-ago land and a faraway time,
There lived an old woman named Aunt Annadine,
Who each Monday morning would take a big sack,
And smooth it and spread it, then in it she'd pack
All manner of things to sell or to trade,
From gliders and spiders and cold lemonade,
To trumpets and crumpets and used teddy bears
Whistles and thistles and small yellow chairs.
Then she'd pick up her bundle and off she would trundle,
Across the creek and be gone for a week
Or until everything was sold, so I'm told.

One day her old husband got terribly mad
And told her, "Doggone it! I think it's right bad
That you get to go out and sell things and play,
While I stay home and keep the house clean every day.
Well, I'm tired of washin' and scrubbin' the floors,
And oilin' the hinges on squeaky old doors!
I wanna go out and have some fun too!
So you listen good to what I'm tellin' you!
The next time you trundle away with your bundle
Across the creek to be gone for a week,
You'll have company, see?
And that company's. . . me!"

Aunt Annadine just smiled and nodded her head
And gave him a wink, and here's what she said:
"I just might be able to trade our old cat,
But inside my pack he'd be squashed and squished flat!
So you're welcome to join me as I go far and near,
If you can carry the cat, my dear!"

"Ha ha! Carry the cat? There's nothin' to that!
He's too little and too light to give me any fight.
I'll pop him in a basket and keep him outa sight.
So pick up your bundle and off we will trundle
Across the creek for all of next week
Or until all the things that you hold. . . are sold!"

So they crossed the creek and traveled for miles,
And the old man's face was covered with smiles
When he saw the huge bundle that on her back sat,
While he just carried a basket that cradled the cat.
When they arrived at the very first town,
Aunt Annadine set her old heavy pack down,
And summoned the people by ringing her bell,
And called out the strange things that she had to sell.

"Hey! I have roses 'n hoses 'n statues of Moses!
Some spices and mices and dishonest dices!
A painting by Rembrandt that might be a phony,

A bony old pony that eats macaroni!
They're all here in my pack; who know when I'll be back?
So do not be shy! Come on, step up and buy!
Come buy-o, come buy-o, come buy-o, come buy!"

And the people came running with money to pay,
And sought things and caught things
  and bought things all day!
Til Aunt Annadine's pack was quite a bit lighter,
While the money swelled her purse tighter and tighter!
Then up stepped an old woman, quite happy and fat,
Who said, "Would you be willing to trade me a cat?

We have a wildcat my husband caught last week.
He weighs thirty pounds, and just in the past week,
He's eaten so much we can no longer feed him!
He's a beautiful cat, but we no longer need him.
So I'll make you a trade, and I'll throw in a dollar,
If you will swap me for one that is smaller!"

Aunt Annadine nodded. The trade then was made,
And into the basket the wildcat was laid.
Aunt Annadine picked up a much lighter pack
And said, as she swung it up onto her back,
"We'll go to the next town; it's really quite near,
If you can carry the cat, my dear!"

"Hmm! Carry *this* cat? Well, not much to that!
He's mean and he's quick, but the basket is thick.
So pick up your bundle and off we will trundle
And sell all you hold for some silver and gold!"

So off they did go to the next little town,
Where Aunt Annadine set her lighter pack down,
And summoned the people by ringing her bell,
And called out the strange things she still had to sell.

"Hey! I have peaches 'n bleaches 'n musical screeches!
Some widgets 'n midgets that come with the fidgets!
Some talkative parrots and some nice tasty carrots!
They're all here in my pack; who knows when I'll be back?
So do not be shy! C'mon, step up and buy!
Come buy-o, come buy-o, come buy-o, come buy!"

So the people bought jams and hams and Spams,
Some candied yams and some deep-fried clams!
And after she'd just sold some butter and lard,
A strange man approached her and gave her his card.

"I'm Mr. Blue, from the zoo. Is it true that you
Have a wildcat or two? Though one would do."
"Why, yes!" Annadine said. "We got one yesterday!
Would you like to buy him? How much will you pay?"

"Oh, I can't pay with money!" the zookeeper said.
"Our budget's too low. But listen! Instead,
I'll make you a trade! Now give me your anther.
Would you swap for a 150-pound panther?"
Aunt Annadine mumbled and thought for a bit,
Then asked, "Do you have a basket a panther would fit?"

"Indeed, I do!" said Mr. Blue from the zoo.
"It's really quite new, it's true, but I'll give it to you!"
And after the panther was all tucked away,
(It took twenty people and half of the day.)
Aunt Annadine said, and her face was all smiles,
"The next village we go to is about fifteen miles!
So come along with me, and be of good cheer,
If you can carry the cat, my dear!"

"Whoa! Carry *this* cat? I dunno about that!
I think I'd rather trundle away with your bundle,
'Cause it's so much lighter 'n this panther's a fighter!
But it's true I must do what I promised to do:
To carry the cat, whether small, big or fat,
Till your bundle is sold and your purse full of gold.
Well, I won't tell you no, but I'll try,
So let's go!"

So off they did go to the third little town,
Where Aunt Annadine set her much lighter pack down,
And summoned the people by ringing her bell,
And called out the few things she still had to sell.

"Hey! I have glasses 'n gasses 'n sticky molasses!
Some pliers 'n briars 'n telephone wires!
Long pointy nails and pails full of snails!
They're all here in my pack; who knows when I'll be back?
So do not be shy! C'mon, step up and buy!
Come buy-o, come buy-o, come buy-o, come buy!"

And after she'd just sold a used feather bed,
Another man stepped up beside her and said,
"My name is Birkus. I work for the circus.
Do you have a panther for sale?
For we own a tiger who comes from Balpiger.
Alas! He's lost half his tail!
We can no longer use him, but don't care to abuse him,
So we'll trade you now, strange though it sounds.
Our tiger's precocious and a wee bit ferocious.
He also weighs 500 pounds!"

Aunt Annadine beamed, but her old husband screamed
And took off running over the hill.
"I might carry a fat cat, but I won't carry *that* cat!

Oh, nosir! Be danged if I will!
Sure, you can trundle away with your bundle
And sell all your stuff here and there.
But while you're out roamin', I'm stayin' at home 'n
Not movin' one inch from my chair!"

And so ends the story of Aunt Annadine,
In that long-ago land and that faraway time.
It began with a cat that she wanted to trade,
And wound up with a curious deal that they made:
She vowed never to ask him to carry the cat,
For when she goes out, he stays home;
And that's that!

Vladimir Boots

In Old Russia, many years ago, there lived a man named Vladimir Boots. He lived in the little village of Footsoreva, on the banks of the River Ug, and Vladimir Boots made — yes — socks! That's right! In his little shop on the banks of the River Ug, Vladimir sewed and spun the softest, smoothest socks you ever slipped your sore feet into.

And why, you might ask, would somebody named Boots make socks? Because right next door to the shop of Vladimir Boots stood the shop of his good friend, Sergei Ivanovich Socks. And Sergei Ivanovich Socks made. . . boots!

Everyone in the little village of Footsoreva knew that Boots' socks and Socks' boots were the finest in the land. And anybody who came to Vladimir Boots for socks would immediately run next door to the shop of Sergei Ivanovich Socks for a pair of fine boots. And those who came to Socks for boots would immediately run next door for a pair of soft, smooth socks from Vladimir Boots!

And if someone came looking for something else, like a coat, Vladimir Boots and Sergei Ivanovich Socks would shake their heads and say:

"We don't make coats. We don't make suits,
But Boots makes socks and Socks makes boots!"

Or, if someone came looking for a locksmith, they would say:

"We don't make keys. We don't make locks,
But Socks makes boots and Boots makes socks!"

Now all went well, until one day a great big man on a great big horse galloped across the River Ug and into the little village of Footsoreva. He wore a big black beard and a great shiny sword, and he had row after row of medals across his chest.

He got down from the big black horse and peered around the little village of Footsoreva until his eye caught the sign that stretched across the tops of the shops of Vladimir Boots and Sergei Ivanovich Socks. It read:

BOOTS & SOCKS

MAKERS OF FINE SOCKS AND BOOTS

The man said, "Hmmm!" and stroked his beard and re-arranged some of his medals. Then he marched into the shop of Vladimir Boots and demanded, "Are you Vladimir Boots?"

"Indeed I am, Sir!" answered Vladimir, trembling just a bit.

"I am Colonel Alexander Alexandrovich Itchibeard! Special courier to His Imperial Highness and Majesty, Czar Nicholas the Not-So-Bright! His Imperial Highness and Majesty needs a new pair of boots. Yours are said to be the finest in the land; so you will come with me!"

And before poor Vladimir could protest, the colonel grabbed him by the scruff of his neck, marched him out the door and tossed him up onto the back of his big black horse!

Then the colonel marched into the shop of Sergei Ivanovich Socks and demanded, "Are you Sergei Ivanovich Socks?"

"Indeed I am, Sir!" answered Sergei, trembling more than just a bit.

"His Imperial Highness and Majesty, Czar Nicholas the Not-So-Bright, has need of a pair of soft, smooth socks to wear under his new boots. Yours are said to be the finest in the land; so you will come with me!"

And with that, the colonel grabbed Sergei by the scruff of his neck, marched him out the door and tossed him up onto the back of the big, black horse, right behind poor Vladimir Boots!

Then the colonel jumped onto the back of the big black horse, seized the reins and galloped out of the little village of Footsoreva, across the River Ug, and down the Imperial Highway to the Imperial Capitol and the Imperial Palace of His Imperial Highness and Majesty, Czar Nicholas the Not-So-Bright!

The czar peered down from his Imperial Throne and said, "Vladimir! I need a new pair of boots! They must be the finest in all the land! You will make them for me!"

"But Your Highness!" said Vladimir. "I cannot!"

"Do you refuse the command of your czar and emperor?"

"Alas!" cried Vladimir. "I am Boots, the poor sockmaker. For boots you need the services of Socks, the fine bootmaker!"

But this was too much for Nicholas the Not-So-Bright to understand. So he did what he always did when he could not understand something, which was quite often. He jumped up and down, raved and ranted, chewed on his beard, and threw things all around the Imperial Throne room!

"Impertinence! Treason! Gross Malfeasance!" he shouted. (He wasn't really sure what any of those words meant, but they sure sounded impressive.) "Take him away and lock him up in the Imperial Dungeons until he agrees to do as I command!"

And so poor Vladimir was hauled off to a dungeon and locked away in a cell.

Then the czar peered down from his imperial throne once more and said, "Sergei Ivanovich Socks, I need your service! All my Imperial Socks have holes in their Imperial Toes! Make me some new ones!"

"Alas!" cried Sergei. "I am Socks, the poor bootmaker! For socks you need the services of Boots, the fine sockmaker!"

And again the czar did not understand. And again he jumped up and down, raved and ranted, chewed on his beard and threw things all around the Imperial Throne room!

"Balderdash! Foofaraw and General Inconsistencies!" he shouted. (And he didn't know what any of those words meant either.) "Take him away and lock him up with his friend! And see that they both have nothing but stale bread and sour pickle juice until they agree to do as I demand!"

And so poor Sergei soon found himself locked away in a cell along with his good friend, Vladimir Boots.

"Alas!" cried Vladimir. "Will we ever again see our beautiful little village of Footsoreva on the banks of the River Ug?"

"Alas!" cried Sergei. "Will we ever again have anything but stale bread to eat and sour pickle juice to drink?"

"Yes!" said Vladimir. "Yes we can, *if* we think and work together!"

So they worked and they thought, stopping only for a little stale bread and sour pickle juice, until at last they had their plan. Then Vladimir called to the guard and said that he was ready to do as Nicholas the Not-So-Bright had demanded. He was taken back to the throne room and brought before the czar.

"I will make the boots, just as you command," he said. "But I will need my assistant to help me. Would you please bring me Sergei Ivanovich Socks?"

"Why do you need an assistant?" asked the czar.

"Why, Your Majesty!" said Vladimir. "Even you, the greatest ruler in all the world, do not carry out your own commands. You use servants and assistants for that. As it is with the greatest ruler, so it is too with the greatest bootmaker!"

"Now that makes sense!" cried the czar. "Let Socks be brought forth!"

So Sergei Ivanovich Socks was brought forth, and Vladimir turned to him and said, "Sergei! Measure His Imperial Highness' Imperial Feet for his new Imperial Boots!"

And Sergei took the measurements, just as he would have if he had been working by himself, and brought them to Vladimir, who pretended to study them, and then said, "Now, cut out the patterns and make the boots just as I have always taught you!"

And all the while that Sergei worked, Vladimir walked round and round his workbench, stroking his beard and muttering, "Hmmmm! Yeeess!" and "Veery Goood!"

And when the boots were finally finished, Vladimir stepped in and applied the final dab of polish to the Imperial Toes. Then he bowed low and presented the boots to the czar.

"Very handsome boots indeed!" cried the czar. "Vladimir, you shall be greatly rewarded! And now, Sergei, will you make me a pair of fine socks?"

"But of course, Your Highness!" cried Sergei Ivanovich Socks. "But I too shall need my assistant!"

Once again the czar said, "Very well." So Sergei turned to Vladimir and said, "Vladimir! Measure his Imperial Highness' Imperial Feet for his new Imperial Socks!"

And Vladimir took the measurements, just as he would have if he had been working by himself, and brought them to Sergei, who pretended to study them and then said, "Very well. Now weave the socks just as I have always taught you!"

And all the while that Vladimir worked, Sergei walked round and round his loom, stroking his beard and muttering, "Hmmmm! Yeeess!" and "Veery Goood!"

And when the socks were finally finished, Sergei stepped in with a huge pair of scissors, and with a great flourish, snipped the final thread. Then he bowed low and presented the socks to the czar.

"Very handsome socks indeed!" cried the czar. "Sergei Ivanovich, you too shall be greatly rewarded!"

And so it was that Vladimir Boots and Sergei Ivanovich Socks received their great rewards and returned to their little village of Footsoreva on the banks of the River Ug, where they continued to make the finest socks and boots in all the land, and to live happily ever after — unless, of course, someone came into their shops hoping to buy — a piano! In which case, they would say:

"We don't make pianos. We don't make flutes.

But Boots makes socks and. . . Socks makes boots!"

The Mousiegator

It was late at night, and all was quiet.
The town was peacefully snoozing away.
It might have been midnight, it might have been later,
When out of the swamp crawled. . . the mousiegator!

Half of him was alligator; half of him was mouse.
He could live out in the swamps;
He could live right in your house!
He was long and green and furry and mean:
A whoopin', snortin' destruction machine!

He got up on his hind legs and wriggled his snout,
And his beady little eyes looked all about.
Then he gave a big grin, and he grinned once more,
And he opened his mouth and he let out a roar!
And he said:

"Whoop-te-do and yahoo! I'm the mousiegator! I can
run faster, jump higher, spit farther, burp louder and
smell badder than any other critter in creation! My daddy
was a thunderbolt and my mama was a streak of lightning, and where I go, plague and devastation just naturally follow! Why, I can eat the eggs and gobble the
cheese and nibble the fuzz off the watchdog's knees!
Whoo-ee!"

Then he moved right in and took over the town,
And every single night when he'd wander up and down,
The people set out baits and traps to catch him,
And all sorts of dogs and kitty cats to snatch him.
But the mousiegator laughed, and wriggled his snout
And kicked up his heels and gave another shout.
And he said:

"Whoop-te-do and yahoo! Do you think I'm a'scared
of you? Why, I'm the mousiegator! I can eat rat poison
by the box and wash it all down with a can of gasoline!
I use mousetraps for earrings, and ride the tornado just
for fun! I'll take on a rattlesnake in my idle moments, and

let him have first bite! Why, I can nibble through walls and break out of jail and tie a big knot in your tomcat's tail! Whoo-ee! I'm long and green and furry and mean! The doggondest sight you ever done seen! Yee-ha!"

"Oh, what can we do?" asked the mayor of the town.

"Oh, what can we do?" prayed the saintly Parson Brown.

"Oh, what can we do?" cried the people with a frown.

"We're afraid that mousiegator's gonna chew
   our houses down!

He's eaten up the dogfood, he's gnawed the kitchen sink,

And he chewed right through the water lines

Just to get himself a drink!

How can a single creature be so doggone
   mean and naughty?

Now no one can take a shower;
   we can't even flush the potty!"

"I've got it!" cried the schoolteacher,
   whose mind was always keener.

"To get rid of someone mean,
   you must get someone who's meaner!

We can solve our little problem with no further muss or fuss,

By sending off a letter to. . . the rumplepussimus!"

The which-a-what-imuss?

"The rumplepussimus!"

52

Just one week later, at the stroke of noon,
(Not one minute later, not a minute too soon.)
The train pulled in, and they heard somebody cuss,
And out of a boxcar jumped. . . the rumplepussimus!

It was the biggest old cat anyone had ever seen!
His eyes shot yellow fire, and his face was mighty mean!
One of his ears was missing,
  and his whiskers were *not* clean!
But his claws were sharp like razors
  and his voice was high and keen!
And he said:

"Meow and oh wow! You folks think
  you've got some trouble?
Well, the rumplepussimus has come on the double!
'Cause I heard a rumor that there might be a fight,
And nothin' in the world is a greater delight!
'Cause I'm tiger, cougar, and a leetle bit of booger!
Made of bolts 'n nuts 'n scrap-metal guts!
Why, a massacaree is my specialty, and I can do three
A'fore breakfast!"

"Ho ho!" the people shouted. "He's just the cat we need!
He'll grab that mousiegator like a sack of chicken feed!
And chaw him up and claw him up and jaw him up, indeed!"
And off they went to watch the mousiegator beg and bleed.

But the mousiegator told them that he wasn't gonna run.
"Naw!" he said, "I'll stick around and have a leetle fun!
You think that you can scare me with some big ol' pussycat?
Why, I'll chew him up and spit him out in
Twenty seconds flat!"

And all the people wondered then, "Whatever shall we do?
Our town may well be ruined
 by the time these two are through!
Sure, we can haul the loser off and bury him like a sinner,
But whichever one it is, how do we get rid of the winner?"

Of all the people in the town, just one stayed calm and cool.
Old Granny Tottem said, "Hmmph! I'm too old to be a fool!
So let them critters scream and shout for all the world to see!
But if they know what's good for them,
They'll keep away from me!"

So all that afternoon as the sun shone bright,
And all the people stayed indoors, a'shiverin' with fright,
The gator stalked the 'pussimus all up and down,
While the 'pussimus followed gator tracks
Clear across the town.

They followed one another across the railroad tracks,
Through all the shops on Main Street, and through

Gardens, huts and shacks.
And no one could really tell for sure,
Just who was chasing whom.
Until, by accident, they met,
In Granny Tottem's living room!

And they looked at each other,
And they looked at each other,
And they *looked* at each other. . .

Until finally the mousiegator throwed back his head and said, "Whoo-ee! They sent *you* to whip the likes of me? Why, I can eat three of you for breakfast on a day when I'm feelin' poorly; and on a good day, I don't think a dozen of you would do! It's lucky for you I'm feelin' merciful today! So just run along home to your mommy. Sonny, don't throw a fit, and come back and see me when you've growed a bit!"

But the rumplepussimus just arched his back and said:

"Are *you* what they're afraid of?
Well, I'll tell ya somethin' true;
I'd send my little nephew to whup the likes of you!
I don't bother with such small stuff; it's beneath my dignity!
So you just run along and, well,
This time I'll let ya be!"

(But the mousiegator huffed and swore
And said he wouldn't flee.)

So they looked at each other,
And they looked at each other,
And they *looked* at each other. . .
And fumed and fussed and waved their claws,
And showed their teeth and snapped their jaws!
But neither one made a move to fight,
And they mighta sat there all through the night;
But old Granny Tottem walked into the room,
And Granny was totin' her big old broom!

And Granny shook that broom at the mousiegator and said,
"Boo! You ugly ol' critter, get outa here! Shoooo! And the
mousiegator scurried back to the swamp as fast as it could go!

Then Granny whacked the rumplepussimus on the bottom
and said, "Scat! Get on outa here, you dirty ol' cat!" And the
rumplepussimus skeedadled!

Now from that day to this — let me tell you on the double —
No mousiegator's ever caused the leastest bit of trouble.
And furthermore, we've never had the leastest little fuss
Or any kind of bother from no rumplepussimus!
And the reason for this is, you see,
Whenever a rumplepussikitty
Or a mousiegator chick gets to thinkin' kinda quick
About doing somethin' bad, then a mousiegator mom

Or a rumplepussidad
Tells about a mean old Granny Tottem,
Who will swat 'em on the bottom,
And scares 'em into being awful. . . good!

Old Cattywampus
(with love and apologies to T.S. Eliot)

Old Cattywampus, that crooked old cat,
Sits in the Kittycorner, happy and fat,
And dreams of days beyond measure or span
When he sailed the seas in his **cat**amaran.

The Kittycorner Inn is just down the alley,
A seedy old bar, and back in the galley

They fry **cat**fish and **cat**tails for kitties to crunch
While Old Cattywampus tells tales for his brunch.

For he was a smuggler! Yes, that is true.
He ran **cat**sup and **cat**nip to old **Kat**mandu!
He's lived more than nine lives, and the reason is that
He could use every wit that pertained to a cat.

For once, when he lived in an elegant home,
He groomed his fur with a great **cat**acomb.
He sailed all seven seas, and I have it on fact,
That he once navigated the Great **Cat**aract!

He fought with the pirates and sailed through the fog.
Why, his exploits would fill an entire **cat**alog!
He survived a typhoon and a great **cat**aclysm,
By repeating his prayers and his old **cat**echism.

For once the sea struck like the blow of a fist,
And his good ship developed a slight **cat**alyst,
Yet ere that boat sank to the cold ocean floor,
His **cat**apult shot him quite safely to shore.

There he sang to his sweetheart and played his guitar
Until he developed a case of **cat**arrh.
So great was his voice, he would get a **cat**call
From all of the kitties on the old **cat**erwaul.

He's been through **cat**astrophes, that I am sure,
But old Cattywampus knows how to endure.
Don't press for details and don't ask him how
Or he'll give you a highly sarcastic "Meow!"

And explain that each life has been such a thriller
That they're planning to build him a great **cat**erpillar,
That will give every detail of every life story,
Each neatly arranged in its own **cat**egory.

So now in the **Cat**skills he **cat**naps and thinks
Or stops in at the pub for a round of free drinks.
And please do not think it is sad or ironic
When he asks you to buy him a large **cat**atonic,

For then he will tell his whole story for you,
And maybe one-tenth of it just might be true.

The Great Chicken Stampede

Let me tell you all about the time I got caught up in the most gosh-awful, gully-stompin', rip-roarin', feather-dustin', chicken stampede that you ever done heard of.

It all happened one fall when we was drivin' the Colonel's big ol' herd down from the summer range to the railhead at Skillet City to be shipped off to market. Them chickens had been a-runnin' wild on the open range all summer, and they was a mighty tough bunch to keep under control.

We had to keep a sharp eye out, and not just for foxes and coyotes. Oh no! There was *two*-legged varmints as well. We knew that old Greasy George and his band of chicken rustlers was lurkin' around somewhere, and there was a rumor that the Drumstick Indians under old Chief Dusty Feather might go on the warpath. So you can bet we was keepin' a mighty sharp eye out on that drive.

Well, son, we took them chickens down through Giblet Gap, up across Rooster-Tail Ridge, and down through Gizzard Gulch, and we finally got 'em forded safe across the Wishbone River and out onto the Great Eggshell Desert.

Now that desert was somethin', son. Just imagine, billions and billions of broken eggshells! All ground up into a gritty powder that blew in your eyes and got in your nose 'n mouth 'n ears. . . till there warn't nothin' you could feel or see or taste or smell but eggshell! But it had to be crossed if'n we was gonna reach the railhead at Skillet City!

Well, we'd been two days and a night out on the Great Eggshell Desert, and the water was a-runnin' low. But we figured we could make Skillet City by sundown the next day, so we bedded down the herd as best we could. They always got skittish when they had to roost out on open ground, but there was nothin' but eggshell powder for miles around!

Our ol' cook had follered us with his big ol' chuck wagon, but he was a big person, and big people and big equipment always made them chickens jumpy. That's why the ol' Colonel always hired us little fellers to work his herds. Why, ol' Honky 'n me could ride right through the middle of 'em without spookin' em the leastest little bit! So me 'n Max 'n the boys rode the point 'n flanks of the herd, while the ol' cook kept way to the rear.

We figured it was the last night on the drive, and we was all lookin' forward to havin' some fun in Skillet City the next day. But I had a funny feelin'. We still had one more night to spend out in the open, and *anythin'* could happen out on the Great Eggshell Desert! I wasn't any too eager when the foreman came round at midnight and told me it was my turn to go on watch.

We'd managed by then to hold off Greasy George and his gang, and ol' Chief Dusty Feather hadn't given us any trouble. It looked like we might make the drive in record time, and the old Colonel'd have a nice big bonus waitin' for us when we reached Skillet City. But I still couldn't shake that feelin' I had.

Howsomever, I kicked off my blankets — actually they was a couple of the cook's old wash cloths that he let me use — and I went to the remuda and saddled up ol' Honky, and I could tell that he sensed somethin' was a brewin' too.

Some of the boys who had just come in from ridin' night herd was gathered round the campfire, warmin' themselves 'n singin' a few chickenboy songs. The cook saved up all his old toothpicks for our campfire, 'cause a toothpick to us would be like a two-foot stick to you.

That campfire sure did look mighty warm 'n invitin', and I was powerful sorry I had to leave it. I took Fritz with me, that there little weenie dog that ol' Max rode, cause, y'see, he needed to do what doggies need to do at night, and the ol' cook got *mighty* upset if he did it on the wheel of his chuck wagon!

Well, son, I didn't much like the looks of the sky that night. I could see clouds a'buildin' up over in the west, and I figured we might be in for a thunderstorm before the night was over. . . and *nothin'* spooks chickens worse 'n thunder 'n lightnin'! So I rode around that herd real easy-like on ol' Honky, leadin' ol' Fritz by the reins, and singin' to them chickens to try 'n calm 'em down. And this is what I sang:

> I ride an ol' Honky; I lead an ol' Fritz.
>
> I herd all them chickens fer a dollar 'n some grits!
>
> It's late in the evenin' an' I am mighty tired.
>
> But if'n ya run off, I'm sure to get fired.
>
> Settle down, little chickens, settle down 'n don't ya roam.
>
> I'm cold 'n I'm hungry 'n a long way from home!

But I don't think nothin' coulda calmed them chickens that night. I could see 'em rufflin' their feathers, 'n I could hear 'em goin', "Cluck, clucka-cluck!" when they shoulda been asleep.

Then all of a sudden a big bolt of lightnin' split the sky wide open! And right after it came the biggest bang of thunder you ever heard! And from that instant, there was no holdin' any of them chickens; it was a stampede!

Just imagine, son! Forty thousand head of chickens! Skeered plumb outa what little wits they had to begin with! Rushin' across the desert in one headlong mass!

Why, the ground shook under their feet, 'n the feathers was a-flyin' everywheres!

I wheeled ol' Honky and Fritz around and headed back to the camp as fast as I could go, all the while a'hollerin', "Stampede!" at the top of my voice. But I doubt if they ever even heard me over the thunder of them eighty thousand drumsticks, and the squawkin' of them forty thousand USDA-approved cacklers that was a'comin' right behind me! I knew I had to get Fritz back to ol' Max a'fore them chickens reached the camp. . . or my best friend and pard would be scrambled like an egg by them thousands of chicken claws a-trompin' 'n a tramplin' all over his poor carcass!

Whew! What a ride that was, son! I put the spurs to ol' Honky like I never had a'fore. And, as for Fritz, why that little weenie dog ran so fast that his hind end done caught up to his front end and passed it! But still, we barely reached the camp in time for ol' Max to swing into the saddle a'fore them chickens came a'poundin' through like an avalanche, and away we went, a'tryin' to head 'em off!"

But after we'd gone about a mile or so beyond the camp, all of a sudden it dawned on me. That there stampede was a'headin' right straight for Skillet City! So I hollers out to Max and the others, "Don't try to stop 'em, Boys! Just keep 'em a'goin' in the direction they's headed! I'll ride on ahead and warn the town!"

And oh, my! Did I ever put the spurs to that goose then! Old Honky went, "Honk!" and flew like he'd never flewed a'fore! But even so, we wasn't more 'n a few minutes ahead of that herd by the time we reached Skillet

City! We flew right down the main street, with old Honky goin', "Honk!" and me a'hollerin', "Clear the street! Stampede a'comin'!"

Then it was on to the railroad yards, where I hollered out to the train crews, "You boys get them boxcar doors open and get them ramps laid down, 'cause you're gonna see chickens loaded faster 'n you've ever seen 'em loaded a'fore!"

And I mean to tell you, them railroad boys jumped to work so fast, you'd a'thought their britches was afire! And it was a good thing they did, 'cause they'd no more got them big freight car doors open and them big loadin' ramps laid down, when that there herd came stampedin' right down the main street of Skillet City! I mean, that street was nothin' but solid chickens for blocks!

It was a good thing that street led right straight to the railroad yards and right to the ramps, 'cause by that time we couldn't have stopped or turned them chickens. . . no way! Why, they poured right through the yards, right up them ramps and into them boxcars so fast that they doggone near tipped them big freight cars clean over! And they wedged themselves in so tight that we couldn't even pull 'em out at the end of the line! Why, we finally hadta *suck* 'em out with a big vacuum cleaner, which also took all the feathers right off 'em and left 'em all ready for processin'!

The old Colonel was so tickled by the way we got them chickens loaded that he told us he wanted them stampeded into Skillet City every year after that!

Well, we didn't much care for that idea. But, hey! That's another story altogether.

Nobody Loves a Rotten Snake

Once upon a time, there lived a snake
By the name of No-Good Ned!
And everyone knew he was nasty clear through;
Or that's what everyone said.
For a snake's reputation, from the dawn of creation,
Has been horrible, wicked and. . . bad!
Since the Garden of Eden, the snake's been a-needin'
A sympathy he just hasn't had!

But now for Ned. . . he had three friends,
And one was Rotten Rod,
The foulest snake that ever crawled
Above or below the sod!
And one day Rodney said to Ned,
"Hehehehehe! I've got an idea for some fun!
We'll sneak with care to the patio where
The big garden party's begun!
And we'll hide in the food, 'till we get in the mood
To give 'em one heckuva fright!
Then we'll pop up like this, and we'll wriggle and hissssss!
And they'll scream for half of the night!"

Now Ned didn't think it was really quite right
To scare folks and be such a pest.
He didn't think so, but he couldn't say no!
Ned just went along with the rest.

So they slithered up a table and hid
In a potato salad bowl,
Where they nibbled some buds and chunks of spuds,
And Rod swallowed a radish whole.
And when a great big lady came along
With a plate full of chicken and cake,
From their salad bed. . . up popped Rodney and Ned!
And the lady went, "Yaaarrrrgghhh! Snaaaaake!"

And then some ladies fainted and some of them screamed,
And some of them said, "Snakes alive!"
But Bok Choy and Mahout, the two chefs, they ran out,
Armed with choppers and cleavers and knives!
And so Rodney and Ned had to run for their lives,
And poor Ned got out just in time!
But Rodney was swollen by that radish he'd stolen,
And whackwhackwhackwhackwhackwhackwhack!
That would be his last crime!

Now you think Ned would learn from the fate of his friend
That sometimes it's best to say no.
But when Horrible Hank wanted him for a prank,
Ned said that he guessed he would go.

"We'll sneak into old McGrew's garden tonight,"
Said Hank, "and will we have a time!
We'll mash the potatoes, then we'll trash the tomatoes,
And we'll cover the turnips with slime!"
Now Ned couldn't handle this being a vandal
But he thought that Hank was his friend.
So though it was wrong, old Ned went along,
To be with his friend to the end.

And Horrible Hank gave a terrible yank,
And down came a whole row of beans!

And poor Ned stood by with a tear in his eye,
While his friend totaled out the mixed greens!

But this horrible snake made a big, bad mistake;
He made too much noise with his fun!
And from the house flew out old Farmer McGrew,
And Old McGrew carried. . . a gun!
So Ned and his friend had to run once again,
As old McGrew's shotgun went boom!
And Ned got away, but I'm sorry to say,
Hank's now stuffed in McGrew's trophy room!

Now, two narrow escapes from two terrible scrapes
Should convince any snake. . . so how come
Ned did it again? Well, I guess it is plain,
Ned wasn't no good! Ned was. . . dumb!

For when his good buddy, who was old Awful Arnie,
Wanted to plunder the nest
Of a falcon named Lee at the top of a tree
That towered above all the rest;
Well, at first Ned said, "I'm not so anxious to climb
To the top of such a tall tree!
And I don't think it's best to mess with the nest
Of a mean old falcon like Lee!"

But Arnie said, "Chicken!" And he was good at pickin'
The names that would make a snake mad.
And so, poor old Ned, by not using his head,
Was once again nasty and bad!
But at the top of the tree, they found out that Lee
Had been waiting there for their arrival!
And Ned spun around and got safe to the ground,
But for Arnie, there was no survival!

He was carried up high — clear into the sky —
By two claws clamped over his liver!
Then Lee let him drop, with a swiiiisssssshhhh and a splop,
From a thousand feet over the river!

Now Ned was a loner. . . his last friend a goner!
He sat down and started to think
How poor Arnie'd been iced and Rodney'd been diced
And Hank shot; it all made him blink.
"Why did I do it? I knew it was wrong!
Why did I let myself go?
Three of my friends came to terrible ends
Because I could not tell them no!"

Well, sometimes the temptation to do something wrong
Might come from your very best friend.
But if this is so, a polite but firm "No!"
Is the only good answer. . . The End!

The Sortalike

You have probably never even heard of a sortalike, much less seen one, because a sortalike is sort of like just about anything. But it's really like nothing at all. . . except itself.

But one day, two children out walking through the woods did happen to come across a sortalike. It was sort of a small sortalike, barely more than a pup or a cub or a colt or a calf or a kitten or whatever it is that you call a baby sortalike. So the boy had no trouble picking it up.

"What is it?" his sister asked.

"I don't know for sure," her brother replied, "but I think it looks sort of like a puppy."

And no sooner had he said this than the sortalike began to squirm and wriggle in his arms. And as it did, its shape seemed to change, and pretty soon it *did* look sort of like a puppy.

"Let me see it!" the girl demanded after her brother had petted it for awhile. She took it and looked at it and said, "I think it looks sort of like a kitten."

And no sooner had she said this, than the sortalike began to squirm and wriggle in her arms. And as it did so, its shape seemed to change again, and pretty soon it did look sort of like a kitten.

Her brother took it back and said, "I liked it better when it was sort of like a puppy." And no sooner had he said this, than the sortalike began to squirm and wrig-

72

gle and change in his arms, until once again it looked sort of like a puppy.

So they took it home with them, taking turns carrying it, and watching it change back and forth from sort of like a kitten to sort of like a puppy and listening to it make strange, "Meowoof!" kinds of sounds.

But when they got it home, their mother wouldn't let it in the house. "Take that thing out of here!" she ordered. "It looks. . . it looks. . . sort of like a rat!"

And no sooner had she said this, than the sortalike began to squirm and wriggle once again, until it did look sort of like a rat! Then it jumped out of the children's arms and ran around the floor, wriggling its whiskers and looking for some cheese to munch on!

"Gaaah!" said the mother.

"Gross!" said the daughter.

"How about that!" said her brother, who sort of liked rats.

"Please!" the girl begged. "Be sort of like a kitten again!"

And no sooner had she said this, than the sortalike became sort of like a kitten again, and jumped back into her arms and began to purr.

"You see?" she said. "It becomes sort of like whatever you want it to be, so I guess we should call it a sortalike. Can we keep it, please? We promise we'll be careful what we say to it!"

"Let's wait till your father gets home," the mother said.

When their father got home that night, he watched the sortalike become sort of like a dog, a cat, a turtle, a squirrel

73

and finally sort of like a canary. But that didn't work out because it couldn't chirp very well.

"Aha!" the father cried. "This could well be the perfect pet! It can be sort of like a horse, when it's outside, that is. We can have it sort of like a watchdog at night. And when it comes time to feed it, we can have it be sort of like a chipmunk or a gerbil! But," he warned, "don't ever say anything about" (and here his voice dropped to a whisper) "an elephant to it! Especially if you're keeping it upstairs in the closet!"

"We won't." the children promised, and then ran outside with the sortalike, which quickly became sort of like a pony and took them galloping off around the neighborhood.

The sortalike quickly became the most popular pet in town. Everybody else wanted one, and everybody went out through the woods looking for one, but nobody ever found one. Apparently this sortalike was the only sortalike in the world, or at least in this one part of it.

So, of course, some people thought about stealing it. But they never could, because whenever anyone like that came around, the children simply changed the sortalike into something sort of like a microscopic bug and hid it away in an empty jar.

Then, when a real burglar broke into their house one night, he found something sort of like a tiger waiting for him, lashing its tail and roaring! The poor burglar was so scared that he jumped right out of his shoes and ran off so fast that his own shadow couldn't keep up with him.

Meanwhile, the children laughed and changed the sortalike back into something sort of like a rabbit. (That was what their parents wanted, because all they had to feed it was carrots, and tigers don't like carrots all that much.)

The sortalike was very easy to care for. When it came time to clean it, the children simply dumped it into a pail of water and told it to be sort of like a fish. After it had swum around for a bit, they told it to become sort of like a sponge. Then they wrung it out and hung it up to dry.

And they took it to school with them on pet day too, which didn't work out very well. Some of the boy's friends took it down by the teachers' lounge and told it to be sort of like a gorilla. The nearsighted principal thought it was the new p.e. teacher and asked if it was ready to coach the football team, while the sortalike said, "Hoo! Hoo!" and ate twenty-seven bananas it had stolen from the cafeteria.

Both children were sent home with a note saying that the sortalike was *never* to come to school again!

One night, when they were all alone, the children had an idea. "Be sort of like a person, so we can talk to you," they said, and the sortalike immediately became sort of like a person.

"It must be great to be a sortalike," the children said.

But the sortalike shook its head.

"No it isn't," it said. "It's really sorta sad."

"Why?" they asked it.

"Because, yes, I can be sort of like everything, but I can't *really* be anything at all!" the sortalike explained. "I have to spend my whole life being what others want me to be. So I can never, ever be what I want to be!"

The children thought about this for awhile. Then they said, "Suppose we were to let you spend half the time being what you want to be, and the other half being what we want you to be. Would that work?"

The sortalike shook its head again.

"It won't work," it said. "I can never be what I want to be unless you let me go, and no one ever lets a sortalike go. You see, they love it too much to let go."

The children thought about this for a long time. Finally, they said, "We're going to let you go."

"You are?" said the sortalike, who had been changed into something like a talking teddy bear while the children thought. "But why? No one has ever let a sortalike go before!"

"We have to," they answered, "because we're sorta like sortalikes too, and we can never really grow up and be what we really want to be, if we keep hold of you!"

"Then take me back to the woods," the sortalike said, and they did.

When they got to where they had first found it, the sortalike said, "Now put me down, turn around, close your eyes and say, 'Sortalike, Sortalike, be what *you* really are!' And when you turn around again, I'll be gone. Then walk home fast, and try not to cry, because you know I'll be happy."

So they put it down, turned around, closed their eyes, and in voices hardly more than a whisper said, "Sortalike, Sortalike! Be what you really are!" There was a rustling in the bushes behind them, and when they turned around again, the sortalike was gone. They smiled, but there were tears in their eyes as well.

It was a long walk home, and a sad one too, because sometimes it hurts to do something, even when it's right.

But when their mother tucked them in that night, she hugged them both extra tight and whispered, "Sortalikes, Sortalikes, be what you really are!"

And there was a smile and a tear on her face too.

The Ballad of Big Ben's Boots

Now there never was a logger like Big Bad Ben!
Stood six-foot-nine, weighed about three-ten!
Bristles on his beard like binder twine,
And legs big around as a lodgepole pine!
His nose jutted out like a big old spur,
And his arms were the size of second-growth fir!
His eyes could freeze you with just one look,
And his hands grabbed and held like a peavey hook!

His personal hygiene wasn't all that good.
Ben didn't take a bath quite as often as he should,
Maybe once a year, twice at the most,
And it had always been Ben's boast
That he'd never once changed his underwear!
When it crumbled away, he'd just add a new pair!
And whether he was sober or whether he was drunk,
Ben's breath smelled like he'd been eatin' raw skunk!
So for reasons that appear to be perfectly sound,
Folks didn't much care to have old Ben around!

There was only one thing that Ben admired,
And that was his boots! And he never got tired
Of cleanin' and rubbin' 'em every night

With mink oil grease, just to keep 'em watertight.
And the caulks on the bottom weren't just little spikes.
They were sharp as needles or miniature pikes!
He could ride the logs with 'em right down the river,
And the folks in town would shake and shiver
When Ben showed up on a Saturday night,
With his boots all polished and lookin' for a fight!

One night, he came lookin' for Fiddler Jim,
Sayin', "I'm gonna do a number on him!
'Cause I don't like to listen to the music of no fiddle,
And watch folks hop around like they gotta run and piddle!"
But the townsfolk told him, "Ben, you came too late!
Old Fiddler Jim has done met his fate.
He's cashed in his chips; he's crossed the divide!
Or to put it more plainly, Old Jim's up and died!"

"Doggone!" said Ben. "That's a rotten thing to do!
Why, I've been up in the woods for a month or two,
Just thinkin' about when I'd meet up with Old Jim,
And all the fun I'd have a'stompin' on him!
Got my boots all polished and ready to kick;
Never thought Old Jim'd pull such a trick!
Why'd he have to go and die thataway?
I'll bet he did it just to ruin my day!"

"Well, he's gone," they told him.
"It's sad, but it's true.
We planted him last Tuesday,
So there's nothin' you can do!"

"Yes there is," said Ben.
"If he's dead, then I expects
To go up to his house and pay my last respects!
I'll just make myself at home." And the townspeople cried,
"You'd stay in the house of a man who's just died?
Why, ain't you got no fear of the dead?"
"Not of old Jim!" was all Ben said.

So Ben walked up the hill to the fiddler's place
With a glint in his eye and a sneer on his face,
Kicked open the door and ambled inside
And stood for a moment, tryin' to decide,
"What should I do? Where should I start?
Should I wreck the place 'n tear it all apart?
Or maybe I cou. . . Hey now! Lookee there!
There's old Fiddler Jim's favorite chair!
Sittin' right next to a fireplace fulla wood!
A nice warm fire'd feel mighty good
On a night like this! Reckon I'll just sit
And warm my tired old feet for a bit!"

So Ben lit the fire and took off his boots,
And took out his flask and took a couple toots!
"Aah!" he said. "This does feel purty good!
Jim, if you could hear me, I'd thank ya; yes, I would!
But I reckon you've gone where we all go — rich or poor —
Still, I wish ya coulda waited till I whupped ya
Just once more!

But lookee here, Jim! Even if you're just a ghost,
I reckon you're bein' a mighty poor host —
Ignorin' your company thisaway —
If ya got a ghostly fiddle, then why don't ya play?"
And Ben gave a laugh, not expectin' no reply,
And lifted up his flask again, 'cause he was kinda dry.
But the room grew colder as Ben took a nip of gin,
And then he heard the music of a ghostly violin!
It seemed to come from someplace way up in the air.
Ben looked all around, but couldn't spot it anywhere.
Then it drifted lower, 'till it danced around his chair.
"Play on!" the logger muttered.
"I ain't movin'! I don't scare!"

The music stopped, and Ben sat a'wonderin'
What would happen next?
Then his left boot gave a little hop,
Just as if it had been hexed.

It hovered in the air a foot or so above the floor,
Then came back down and everything was silent as before.
Then the right boot arose, like the left one had done.
Old Jim's ghost, it seems, was plannin' a little fun!
Somethin' gave a little twitch, down at the toes,
And then the laces tied themselves in neat little bows.
Ben's face got red, and when he spoke,
His voice was cold and flat.
"You've done put on my boots!" he said.
"No ghost gets away with that!"

The music started up again,
And the boots began to dance.
Ben stood there a'watchin' 'em
Like a man stuck in a trance.
But then he arose again, straight like a tree.
Calculatin' as he did where Jim's chin oughta be!

Ben threw a punch that woulda killed
Most anyone, anywhere —
Anyone alive, that is —
But all Ben hit was air!
Then one boot rose high, and those needle-sharp caulks
Came down with a crunch on Ben's smelly socks!
"Show yerself!" Ben hollered,
"Come on and fight me fair!"
But Jim remained invisible, just like a puff of air.

Ben's other foot got stomped, and before he could begin
To yell, a boot drew back and kicked him in the shin!

Ben grabbed his shin and yelled with rage,
Snarled like a wildcat caught in a cage,
Hopped on one leg around the floor,
And then that boot drew back once more
And kicked his other shin and then,
Up went that leg, and down went Ben!
Flat on his stomach with a thump and a whack,
And the boots came down on the small of his back!

The music started up again, and old Ben swore
As Jim's ghost started in to dance once more.
A quick little jig up and down Ben's spine,
Always to the music and always in time.
Then the boots came down with a whack and a thump,
And a one-two stomp on poor Ben's rump!
"Enough!" Ben hollered. "I've got sense enough to know
When I've been whupped; lemme up 'n I'll go!"

So Ben ran out of the fiddler's house
And down the hill like a scared little mouse!
Ran through the town in his stockin' feet,
And all the townsfolk watchin' had themselves a treat
When they saw them boots a'chasin' him,

And at every single jump,
They'd land another kick on Ben's battered rump!

Maybe it was fitting, and I think it kinda suits.
Y'see, Ben was kicked outa town. . .
With his very own boots!

The Hairiers
(or why men go bald)

Now why do you suppose men lose their hair?
It hardly ever happens to a dog or a bear.
Some people don't know and others don't care,
But I'm here to tell you why it's thin up there.

It's the hairiers that are responsible: funny little critters about two or three inches tall. Bet you've never even heard of 'em.

But the hairiers are what they're called,
And what they want is to steal you bald!
They won't be stopped, and they won't be stalled.
They'll swipe your hair and off it's hauled. . .

Off to wherever it is they haul it. Now, nobody really knows for certain where that is. Nobody but me!

But maybe I shouldn't be doin' this song.
Maybe I'm comin' on a little too strong.
Y'see I thought folks knew all along
Who the hairiers are, but maybe I'm wrong.
So I'll stop this rhyme and tell you all about 'em!

The story begins long, long ago, in the days before days were numbered or named, when the wild beasties roamed the hills and men stayed safe in the valleys, when critters were around that aren't around any more: all kinds of critters, big ones and small, fierce ones and tame, odd ones and ordinary. But perhaps the oddest of all were the hairiers.

Of course, they weren't called the hairiers back then. I don't know just what they were called — probably something like "Uuugghh!" or "Eeeeef!" or "Aaaagg!" — because this was a very long time ago indeed. But they were little critters, just a couple of inches high, and covered all over with hair, except for their eyes and their hands and their feet; and they had three each of those!

I'm not sure how they lived or what they ate back in the days before days were numbered or named, but I think I do know how they happened to come to be called the hairiers.

You see, these little critters were very shy and tried their best to stay away from men, and usually they were pretty good at keeping out of sight. But one winter, when the winds were cold and the snows were deep, one of these little critters found himself sharing a cave with a caveman, and his cavewife.

Everything went fine, as long as the little critter stayed hidden out of sight at the back of the cave, and the caveman did not even know he was there. But the winds were so cold and the snows were so deep, that the poor little critter couldn't go outside to forage for food. So one night he crept up to the fire where the caveman lay snoring after dinner, and he tried to steal a scrap of leftover meat.

Only he wasn't quite quick enough!

"Neeerrggh! cried the caveman as he grabbed the little critter with his big, thick hand. "What this?"

"Let me go! Please let me go!" squeaked the little critter. "All I want is a bite to eat and a chance to warm myself at your fire!"

"Uuuuh! You want warm? I make warm!" said the caveman. And with that, he held the poor little critter right over the fire, and turned him this way and that, until the flames had singed all his hair away!

Then the caveman laughed again and said, "You too warm now! I make cold!" And with that, he threw the poor little critter right out of the cave and into the snow! Then the caveman lay back down beside the fire and began to snore.

Well, I suppose the poor little critter would have frozen out there, but the cavewife felt sorry for it. So she took a knife, cut a piece from a fur that was lying around, and took it, along with some food, out to where the poor little critter lay shivering in the snow. She fed it and wrapped it and warmed it gently until the poor little critter felt just a bit better.

So all through that winter, the little critter lay hidden in the back of the cave, trying to think of a way to get even with the caveman, while it waited for its hair to grow back out again; but it wouldn't grow back out again! So the poor little critter stayed completely bare!

One night, the little critter crept up to the fire where the caveman lay snoring, and he thought and he thought and he *thought!*

"He's much too big for me to hurt," the little critter decided. "But I bet if I took hold of one of the hairs on his head, and pulled real careful-like with all three hands, I bet, I just bet, I could pull it. . . out!"

And out it came!

The caveman said "Ummmmph!" in his sleep, but he didn't wake up! So the little critter took hold of another hair on the caveman's head, and pulled real careful-like, and out *it* came! Then he pulled out another, and then another, and then another still!

After a time, the little critter crept back to its little hiding place in the back of the cave and tried to think of just what it could do with this handful of hair it had pulled from the caveman's head. First he tried twisting them, but that didn't accomplish anything. Then he tried making knots, but that didn't do any good either. Then he laid them out in rows, side by side, and began working at them with all three hands; by daylight, the little critter had invented weaving!

First he wove himself a little shirt with three arms. Then the next night he went back and stole some more hair, and started work on a trio of trousers! (He couldn't very well make a *pair* of trousers if he had three legs now, could he?) A few nights later he went back for some more hair, and started work on a set of slippers. By the end of the winter, the little critter had four complete outfits for himself, and the caveman had a big bald spot on the top of his head!

"What happen my hair!" he cried, but he never found out. "My hair; it all go 'way!"

The little critter heard him shouting about his lost hair and began to think of himself as. . . a hairier! So that's what he became.

Sometimes, when he crept up by the fire at night, the little critter was tempted to steal some of the cavewife's hair too. But he remembered how kindly she had treated him, so he left her hair alone. Maybe she suspected what was going on, but she never said anything about it!

At last the snows melted and the winter came to an end, and the little critter was able to leave the cave and go back to its own tribe once again. And they were all so impressed with his new outfits that they decided to singe all their hair off too, and get themselves clothes just like him!

"But!" the first hairier told them, "you must only take the caveman's hair! Leave the cavewife's hair alone. . . because it was a cavewife who saved my life!"

And they all promised to do this, and so they have continued right down to this very day!

But, you may wonder, why is it they only take *some* men's hair, and not others? Well, over the years — hundreds of years, thousands of years, tens of thousands of years — these little critters have become very particular! They won't take just anybody's hair, only the best! If you know someone who's losing it (like the guy who wrote this book), that is because the hairiers think it is first-rate, top-notch, grade-A, number one USDA-grade and approved prime hair! And that is the reason why some of us are being clearcut.

Now, if we could only teach them how to practice reforestation.

But they are still so shy and they live so far down —
under the bed and under the rug and under the floor and
under the house and under the earth — that they are
dang-nigh impossible to find! And they have become so
good over the years at pulling out your hair without
waking you up, that you don't even realize they're har-
vesting you until most of it is gone!

But how did I find out. Well, I have to go back to the
rhyme for that:

> One night, I just pretended to sleep.
>
> I lay right still, and I didn't make a peep.
>
> And just after midnight I heard 'em creep
>
> Up from their hideouts, way down deep!

Under the bed and under the rug and under the floor
and under the house and under the earth; that's where
they come from!

> Old Dig-'Em-Out Dan was their boss man.
>
> He could steal your hair quick as anybody can!
>
> He always had a scheme, and he always had a plan;
>
> Weren't nobody slicker than the clan Dan ran!

Only they weren't quite slick enough for me! Quick as
a wink and a blink, I grabbed a'hold of old Dan and
asked him just what he thought he was doing a mess-
ing around with my head!

And here's what he said:

"We need new overalls for my brother Tom,
And a new winter coat for my poor old mom,
And my teenage daughter wants a dress for the prom!
So I'm hoping you'll be nice and calm. . .

"And let us take just a few more. Can't hardly do you any harm now, can it? And it's such fine quality hair! Can't scarce find any better in the whole dadburn county!"

Well, what could I say? Could I let his poor old mother freeze that winter? Could I let his little girl go to the big dance in a dress made out of *second-rate* hair? And how could his poor old brother work without good overalls?

I told him to go ahead, and I don't mind, since all my hair is going for a good cause. And I think I'm in pretty good company, because:

You'll notice that _____ is on their list.
And _____ sure hasn't been missed!
And _____ is losing a few.
Why they might even be getting _____ too!

(Fill in the blanks with anyone anywhere,
who has a *quality* head of hair.)

91

The Song of Cobalt Blue

Yessir, son, there never was and never will be a hound dog to compare with old Cobalt Blue! I remember the day he first arrived at our house; came in five different kits from ABCD Inc. (Acme Brand Computerized Doggies, Inc.)

Grandpappy built him with the ears of a wolf, the nose of a bloodhound, the jaws of a bulldog, the body of a great Dane and the legs of a greyhound. He also added a telescopin' aluminum tail that you could pull out to where it was more'n eight foot long, and which served as a radio antenna, and which also went whap! whap! whap! when he wagged it on the hearth.

Grandpappy built old Cobalt Blue 'specially to hunt down the wild whoopees that lived in the Great Polyester Forest that stretched away beyond our farm. Now that forest was sure somethin', son. Mile after mile of big plastic trees, all covered with Velcro bark and nylon leaves or acrylic needles! And parts of it was full of polyurethane fiber-fill underbrush! Took quite a hound dog to hunt in a place like that, especially if he was chasin' after the wild whoopees, which were the hardest synthetic critters in the world to catch.

You see, the designer who built the prototypes didn't know what sort of legs to put on 'em, so he put on two sets, four on the front and four on the back. So when them critters got tired of runnin' on one set of legs, they'd just flip themselves over and run on the other set!

Them wild whoopees, y'see, was 'sperimental critters that got loose from the lab and ran into the Great Polyester Forest and lived there and multiplied. And after a time, they got so bold that they'd sneak down out of that forest at night, right down into our fields, where they would proceed to steal all the candy-coated peanuts and popcorn right off'n our Cracker Jack bushes! Why, a couple of 'em even broke into the barn one night and took all the low-cholesterol, non-dairy creamer right out of Grandma's artificial cow! We even caught one in the henhouse, swipin' the tofu eggs right out from under our soybean chickens!

93

It was right at this point that Grandpappy decided that somethin' had to be done. So as soon as he got old Cobalt Blue assembled, we took him straight down to the ADRS (Automatic Doggie Repair Shop), put him up on the hoist, and had a special set of five wide, steel-belted radial paws installed, four on his legs and a spare for his trunk, in case he had a blowout. And in the winter, when the land was covered with ice and snow, we'd just take ol' Cobalt Blue into the ADRS, put him back on the hoist, take off his regular paws and put on a set of studded snow paws!

That very afternoon when we got ol' Cobalt Blue back from the ADRS, we heard them wild whoopees just a-whoopin' and a-hollerin' down in the Cracker Jack patch. "By thunder!" says Grandpappy. "It's time we taught them critters a lesson! C'mon, Ol' Cobalt, we're goin' huntin'!"

Ol' Cobalt Blue just reached up and licked Grandpappy's face with his big ol' tongue, which, by the way, was a kinda sponge that could unroll out to where it was more'n four foot long. This meant that he could also lick the gravy outa the bottom of the pan on the stove without even gettin' up on his hind legs to do it!

So we took ol' Cobalt Blue out back, topped off his tank with unleaded supreme, made sure his huntin' teeth were set in tight; he had three sets of teeth, y'see. Stainless steel for huntin', hard plastic for eatin', soft rubber for playin', so's he wouldn't hurt the little kids none if he nipped 'em any.

Them there wild whoopees just whooped and hollered when they saw us a 'comin'. They figured they was gonna have another easy time of it. But Grandpappy punched in the *hunt* command on his remote control panel, and ol' Cobalt Blue started to trot. Then he activated the voice module, and ol' Cobalt Blue gave a howl, the likes of which has not been heard a'fore or since! Y'see, Grandpappy had made a three-track stereo recordin' of an old-time locomotive whistle, a fire siren and a foghorn! So ol' Cobalt Blue, when he howled, could go, "Twooot!" and "Ruuuurrr!" and "Beeeeeyooooo!" all at the same time!

It was at this point them wild whoopees realized they had more than the average computerized doggie to deal with! So they started makin' tracks back to the forest. Then Grandpappy punched in the *get 'em!* command, and ol' Cobalt Blue's steel-belted radial paws spun so fast that they smoked; he laid a strip of rubber that was forty feet long! At the same time, his afterburner cut in, and a big ol' flame shot out of his. . . weeelll. . . tailpipe!

I can tell you that two of them big wild whoopees didn't make it back to the forest that afternoon! By the time we could catch up to him, ol' Cobalt Blue had scrambled their circuits and mangled their microchips! All we could salvage was some scraps of hide for Grandma to use for cleanin' rags.

It was at this point that Grandpappy wrote the first verse to his song about ol' Cobalt Blue, and it went:

I built a dog name of Cobalt Blue.
Chases them whoopees down, two by two.

He can catch anything in or out of the zoo.

He caught everything except the flu!

Singin' heeere, ol' Cobalt Blue;

You're a good synthetic hound dog, you!

Now, after about two or three weeks of this, them wild whoopees' numbers was beginnin' to diminish considerable, and we was lookin' forward to havin' one of the bestest Cracker Jack crops in years! Ol' Bossie was givin' the bestest low cholesterol, non-dairy creamer any artificial cow ever produced! And our soybean chickens was layin' the bestest tofu eggs you ever sunk your teeth into. Every afternoon or evenin' ol' Cobalt Blue would go huntin', and one or two more of them wild whoopees would bite the silicon dust, till there warn't more than one left!

But this last great wild whoopee was the wiliest old so-and-so that you ever saw; or rather, that you *never* saw. That was the problem. He was too smart to come out of the forest, 'cept late at night, when he'd just make a quick dash down into the field and rip up a Cracker Jack bush or two. And if we waited for him there, he'd circle up by the barn and steal a few quick swallers of low-cholesterol, non-dairy creamer outa ol' Bossie. And by the time we heard her bawlin' and headed back to the barn, he'd be on his way back to the forest. All we could do was listen to him goin' "Whoopee! Whoopee! Whoopee!" as he went.

He was some kinda traveler too, son, 'cause he had sixteen legs instead of eight! He had four on the front, four on the back and four on each side! He used one set to run, one set to jump, one set to climb and one set to swim! And he had two heads: one on each end! That meant you could never sneak up on him from behind, because there warn't no behind to sneak up on!

When he reached that forest, he'd run 'n jump 'n climb 'n swim 'n double 'n triple 'n quadruple back on his trail till the bestest hound dog ever programmed couldn't catch up to him! Ol' Cobalt Blue got to feelin' so dang flusterpated — that's a combination of flustered and exasperated — at not bein' able to catch that last great wild whoopee that Grandpappy hadta write another verse to his song, and it went:

Ol' Blue tried and he tried so hard,

Chased that whoopee all over the yard!

Wore out four sets of radial paws,

But he couldn't get close to that whoopee's claws!

Singin' heeere, ol' Cobalt Blue!

Yer still a good synthetic hound dog, you!

But despite them encouragin' words, ol' Cobalt Blue started pinin' away outa sheer flusterpation at not bein' able to catch that last great wild whoopee. First he stopped lickin' the gravy outa the bottom of the pan on the stove. Then his tongue got all dried and cracked, and he knocked and he pinged when we topped off his tank. Pretty soon, he took to just lyin' around and not even barkin' at the wind-up cats any more!

It was at this point that Grandpappy started sittin' 'n thinkin' 'n thinkin 'n sittin' 'n sittin' 'n thinkin' until finally he got an idea. He called up a friend, who called up a friend, who called up a friend, who called up a friend, who had a friend who worked for the Department of Defense!

About a week later, a strange-lookin' package arrived at the farm! Came from the Pentagon and it had *Top Secret* stamped all over it! Grandpappy grabbed it and ol' Cobalt Blue and headed straight down to the Automatic Doggie Repair Shop!

When we got ol' Cobalt Blue back from the ADRS the next day, there was a strange new look in his eye. All afternoon long he sat around, whappin' his aluminum tail on the hearth and starin' out through the window across the fields to the Great Polyester Forest, where he knew the last great wild whoopee was a' waitin', waitin' for dark so's he could come and raid the farm again!

Pretty soon the sun began to go down, and we took ol' Cobalt Blue out to a special pad by the barn to wait. After a time, ol' Cobalt Blue's ears pricked up, and then his nose began to snuff, snuff, snuff! And he began to whine and tug at his leash.

But Grandpappy said, "Not yet, Ol' Cobalt! Let him get a leetle mite closer!"

Soon all of us could hear that last great wild whoopee creatin' all kinds of noise and fuss down in the Cracker Jack patch. "Stand clear!" Grandpappy warned, and then he began his countdown. "Ten! Nine! Eight! Seven! Six! Five. . . we have main engine ignition! Three! Two! One! Get him!"

And with a roar that shook the barn and trailin' a sheet of orange flame behind him, ol' Cobalt Blue left the launchin' pad and headed straight for the Cracker Jack patch! That there wild whoopee took off as fast as his sixteen legs could carry him, but this time, son, there'd be no escape!

"Y'see," Grandpappy chuckled, "that there friend of a friend of a friend done sent us a heat-seekin' guidance system from outa one of them big air-to-ground missiles! That there wild whoopee can twist and turn and duck and dodge as much as he wants! Ol' Cobalt Blue's locked on, and he's gonna stay locked on till he runs that critter down and nails him!"

Grandpappy was still chucklin' when the phone call came. It was that friend of a friend of a friend. He listened for a spell, and he wasn't chucklin' no more when he hung up the phone.

"I gotta call ol' Cobalt back!" he said. "They done sent us the wrong system! This here one's got a warhead attached to it. When ol' Cobalt hits that whoopee, he's a' gonna go. . . *he's a' gonna go. . .*"

BOOM! It was too late! The explosion was way out in the middle of the forest, but strong enough to rattle the windows. Ol' Cobalt Blue had caught up to that whoopee at last!

Well, we found the spot the next day. The explosion had blown down one hundred and twenty-six plastic trees, and there was nothin' left of that polyurethane fiberfill underbrush 'cept some scorched lint! All we ever found of ol' Cobalt Blue was his huntin' teeth, stuck fast in a piece of one of them sixteen legs of that last great wild whoopee!

Grandpappy never built another dog after that, but here's the last verse of the song that he wrote:

Ol' Blue died with a great big boom;

Glad it didn't happen in the livin' room!

He's a doggone dog, and that's fer shore!

Song's all over, can't sing no more!

Singin' Heere, ol' Cobalt Blue!

You was a good synthetic hound dog, you!

Sam Samson's
Simulated Sheep

"**S**am supplies sheep, sly sheep, shy sheep.
Sam sells swell sheep; Sam says smell sheep. . . aagh!
Sheep smell so strong. . . so says Sam's song,
Sheep! Sheep! Sheep!"

Such was the song Sam Samson sang to summon his simulated sheep, and so starts the strange saga of Sam Samson, the super synthetic sheepherder of the South Central Swanee Slough. Surely you've seen signs saying, "Select Sam Samson's Surefire Simulated Sheepskin Seatcovers, 'specially suitable for your Chevrolet, Saab or Subaru?"

Well. . . .

Sam Samson started simply, as a second-hand sheep seller, selling second-hand sheep to the settlers in the small, scraggly scattered settlements between Sioux City and Saginaw. But Sam Samson soon saw a second-hand sheep seller could scarcely scrape a salary of seventy-six cents in sales between Sunday and Saturday, selling second-hand sheep to the settlers in them small, scraggly scattered settlements struggling to survive between Sioux City and Saginaw.

So Sam sold his second-hand sheep to Simon Simonson, a speculator in second-hand sheep stock and securities from Seattle, with subsidiaries in Sacramento and Spokane, and started for the South Central Swanee Slough, where someone said simulated sheep grew sleek and sassy on the soybeans, sorghum and sassafras that sprouted among the sycamores, cedars and cypresses in that soggy, sloggy slough.

But, Sam Samson soon saw, the South Central Swanee Slough was also full of snigglesnakes! Sly, scaly, sneaky serpents that slithered down the sides of the sycamores, cedars and cypresses and stalked Sam Samson's simulated sheep, striking at their sides and shanks and causing them to shed their synthetic skins too soon! Sam Samson sat on a sycamore stump and sobbed when he saw his simulated sheep shivering and shuddering in that soggy, sloggy slough without their synthetic skins to save 'em from the skeeters and the snigglesnakes that snipped and snapped at their sides and shanks.

"Surely I must save my sheep!" Sam Samson said suddenly, and seized a sycamore stick and a cedar switch and started swinging. He swatted and slapped and smacked and spanked them sly, scaly, sneaky serpents so savagely he scattered 'em from Savannah to Sausalito! By sundown Saturday at seven, the South Central Swanee Slough was once again safe for Sam Samson's simulated sheep to savor the soybeans, sorghum and sassafras in safety, and so Sam solved his first serious situation!

By Sunday, September sixth, Sam saw seven-score simulated sheep all set for shearing. But Sam Samson soon saw that simple, unsophisticated sheepshearers were strangers to simulated sheep, and simply couldn't shear 'em sufficiently or safely. "Slipshod sheepshearing sends shivers shootin' straight down my spine!" Sam said savagely. Y'see, y'shear a simulated sheep skin and all, and the simulated sheep simply starts sprouting a second synthetic skin! So Sam started Sam Samson's South Central Swanee Sheep Shearing Seminary, where selected students from seventeen southern states assembled to study the science of shearing simulated sheep in special, semester-long seminars! Soon Sam saw seven semis stocked with simulated sheepskin seatcovers, all set to send to the salesmen from Chevrolet, Saab and Subaru!

Still, Sam seemed sad and sorrowful, staying single and solitary, surrounded by a soggy, sloggy slough, and subsisting on simple snacks of soybeans, sauerkraut, strawberries, succotash, sesame seeds and sarsaparilla soda. So Sam switched his socks, shined his shoes and set off to see his sweetheart, Sarah Sally Susie Spraggs!

But Sarah Sally Susie Spraggs was smugly and snugly settled in Saskatoon, Saskatchewan, and simply couldn't stand the sight of the South Central Swanee Slough or the smell of Sam Samson's simulated sheep.

"Sheep stink!" Sarah Sally Susie Spraggs said succinctly. "Sheep also sweat and snore from sunset to sunup! How should I sleep softly and sweetly, surrounded by sevenscore snoring, sweating, stinking sheep?"

So Sam simply said, "So long!" to his sweetheart, Sarah Sally Susie Spraggs, who (as her stepsister Sadie sadly shoveled snow) sat smugly and snugly on a sofa in Saskatoon, Saskatchewan, sewing shirts and studying Shakespeare and still saying Sam's sheep stink!

One Sunday, Sam saw a sign saying, "Sheepmen! See who has the Swiftest Sheep in these several Southern States! Select your speediest sheep and start them in the Second Straight Southern Sheep Sweepstakes! Several special certificates and some selected, silver-plated, sapphire-studded spittoons will be sent to the sheepmen possessing the swiftest sheep in these several Southern States!"

"Shucks!" Sam Samson said sadly. "My simulated sheep are so slow, I could set 'em to race a squad of six sick snails, and they'd still finish second! Say! Suppose it's possible to soup up a simulated sheep? Surely, a supercharged, stimulated simulated sheep should sweep the other simple sheep to the sidelines, and I should savor the success of a special certificate. . . and a selected, silver-plated, sapphire-studded spittoon to set by the sofa in my study!"

So Sam started scheming, and studying several sets of specific specifications as he sought the spare sections necessary to assemble his supercharged, stimulated, simulated sheep. Sam schemed and sweated and swore and smirked — and smoked several suspiciously smelly seegars — as he sought the spare sections necessary, and by Sweepstakes Saturday, Sam saw a stable of supercharged, stimulated, simulated sprinting sheep. . . all set to circle the circuit!

At the starter's signal, Sam Samson's supercharged, stimulated sprinting sheep shot down the straightaway so swiftly, the other simple sheep were swept aside. Soon not a single sheep save Sam Samson's supercharged, stimulated simulated sprinting sheep could be seen scurrying and scampering around the circuit. Yessir,

Sam Samson's supercharged, stimulated simulated sprinting sheep swept to a sweet success in them Second Straight Southern Sheep Sweepstakes; but them stupid, silly, synthetic so-and-sos didn't have the sense or the savvy to stop!

So swiftly did they circle the circuit, shooting up the straightaways and sprinting down the stretches, that they simply sprinted straight outa their synthetic skins! And still they kept on sprinting, shedding section after section of themselves, till there simply wasn't a single section of a single supercharged, stimulated simulated sprinting sheep left to shed!

Sam Samson stood stock still in shocked silence. Some scorched sections and singed strips of synthetic skin alone survived of his supercharged, stimulated simulated sprinting sheep. So Sam simply shrugged his shoulders and selected his special certificate and circular, silver-plated, sapphire-studded spittoon, which now sits by the sofa in his study in the South Central Swanee Slough. And so the strange saga of Sam Samson simply and suddenly stops!

The Plain Princess:
A Fairy Tale of Sorts

Long ago and far away, there lived and ruled a king whose only daughter was not beautiful. It seems impossible, but it was so. Her Royal Highness, Princess Penelope Persephone (Princess Penny, for short) was plain. From the time she was a little girl, it was obvious that she would never be all that attractive.

Her hair was neither the color of sunlight upon spun gold nor black as the night on a raven's wing, not even red like the firelight mingling with the sunrise. It was, instead, a dull mousy brown, and it wouldn't even curl!

Her eyes were neither the color of the clear summer sky nor grey-green like the misty sea. They too were a dull brown, and they often squinted, as the princess was a bit nearsighted.

But the eyes were kind and intelligent, and under the dull, stringy hair was a brain that absorbed knowledge more quickly than the finest blotting paper could soak up an ink spill. Indeed, the princess was remarkably clever at many things, though she did get the hiccups every now and then and sometimes forgot her manners and burped at the dinner table.

Her father the king did not notice this at first. Indeed, the king hadn't really noticed his daughter at all for several years. This was not to be wondered at, since Princess Penny's father was King Ambrose the Absent-Minded, who sometimes had trouble remembering which kingdom he reigned over.

One evening at the Royal Supper Table the king did happen to notice his daughter (after the princess had just belched rather loudly). "Pray tell me," he said, "just who is that small, plain, insignificant creature who sits down to dinner with us?"

The queen, Ena the Easily Embarrassed, was too mortified to reply. But the Royal Remembrancer, whose duty it was to remember such things and remind the king of them, said, "That, Sire, is your daughter, the Princess Penelope Persephone."

"Is she, indeed?" asked the king. "She does not look much like a princess. Aren't princesses supposed to be beautiful?"

"It is customary," replied the remembrancer, whose job it was to agree with the king, whether he was right or not.

"Then do something about it," said the king. "Send her to school. Surely there is a proper training school for princesses around here somewhere!"

"Immediately, Sire!" said the remembrancer, and so it was that Princess Penny was enrolled at Madame Flavia's Finishing School for Princesses and Other Royal Persons of Quality.

"Oh dear!" said Madame Flavia at the first sight of her newest pupil. "Send for a tutor! She'll have to start in the remedial class!"

So Princess Penny began at the very beginning. The tutor's first task was to get her to walk daintily in silk slippers set with gold and precious gems. Unfortunately, Princess Penny couldn't walk daintily. Instead, she clumped.

"You must not clump!" the tutor insisted. "Someday you will wear glass slippers set with diamonds. You cannot clump in glass; it breaks!"

"But I don't want glass slippers!" protested Princess Penny. "I don't want any kind of slippers! They are of no practical use and they pinch my feet! Why can't I wear boots instead?"

"What would a princess do with boots?" sneered the tutor.

"They are very handy for hiking through pastures," answered Princess Penny, "especially if one happens to step in cow droppings. And they are useful for fishing as well."

"Princesses do not fish!" cried a shocked tutor. "Nor do they hike through pastures, with or without cow droppings! Those are tasks for varlets!"

"I really don't care to be a princess," Penny decided. "May I please be a varlet instead? It would be far less trouble."

"Impossible!" cried the tutor. "We'll move on to the next lesson: How to Swoon Properly."

"What does that mean?" asked Princess Penny.

"To faint in a manner becoming a princess," said the tutor. "The entire reputation of a Princess may likely depend upon how well she can perform the Royal Swoon."

"It strikes me as being a very useless and silly thing to do," replied Princess Penny, who was used to stomping on snakes and baiting her own fish hooks.

"Perhaps a demonstration will inspire you," said the tutor. He summoned Princess Allison Angelica, Madame Flavia's fairest and most promising student, and two young would-be knights from a nearby Academy for Young Royal and Semi-Royal Gentlemen.

"Be so good as to show us how you fight for the hand of a princess," he told the two aspiring knights. "But please take care not to slay each other. This is only a demonstration."

The aspiring young knights, Roderick and Wolfram, needed no urging. They both had come armed with sword and buckler. They both thought Princess Allison Angelica to be the fairest princess in the world, and they didn't care much for each other to begin with. The room quickly resounded with the clash of sword upon buckler as the two aspiring knights set about the task of trying to carve each other into cutlets.

Princess Allison Angelica covered and then uncovered her eyes, waved her handkerchief and cried, "Oh! Ooh! Oooooh!" The last "Oooooh!" was a perfect D over high C, which she managed to hold for a full seven seconds. Her bosom, set off by a very low-cut gown, throbbed alarmingly. Princess Allison Angelica was very proud of her bosom and how it could throb.

Princess Penny, meanwhile, was studying each fighter's style and form. Roderick, she noticed, fought completely flat-footed, while Wolfram carried his buckler way too low and had a very weak backhand stroke.

"Ooooooooooh!" cried Princess Allison Angelica, this time hitting E over high C and holding it for a full eight seconds with almost no vibrato.

"Get up on your toes, Roderick!" urged Princess Penny. "Move to the left, Wolfram! Hold your buckler higher!"

The combat ended suddenly when Wolfram missed completely with a very clumsy backhand. Roderick, still flat-footed, managed to skewer him between the elbow and shoulder of his sword arm. The sword dropped from Wolfram's hand and he collapsed with a groan, blood running down his arm.

That was Allison Angelica's cue. With a shriek that rose and fell a full two octaves, she clasped one hand over her throbbing bosom (which had already been throbbing spectacularly for nearly two minutes), spun three times counterclockwise — the preferred direction — then collapsed in a flutter of skirts and petticoats.

It was a beautiful swoon, but Princess Penny did not try to copy it. Instead, she whipped a small, sharp knife from a sheath on her belt, cut a strip from the bottom of her own petticoat, wrapped it quickly around Wolfram's injured arm, then used the sheath to tighten it into a very effective tourniquet. The bleeding stopped almost immediately.

"Get some hot water and bandages!" Princess Penny commanded. But Allison Angelica lay in a swoon on the floor. Roderick knelt by her side, holding her hand in the approved manner and murmuring, "Alas, Fair Princess! Have I overwhelmed thee?"

The tutor fluttered around them crying, "Kneel on the other knee, Roderick! Rub her hand gently and speak a bit louder!"

It was all, Princess Penny decided, remarkably silly.

"Hold this just so," she commanded Wolfram, placing his left hand on the sheath. "Loosen it every few minutes. I'll try to find something to bandage it with."

Princess Penny ran to the kitchen for a pan of hot water. When she returned, Princess Allison Angelica still lay in a swoon. "If you won't help one way, you can help in another," Penny decided. And with that, she cut a bandage from the bottom of Allison Angelica's petticoat.

It was made of fine silk, so Penny decided to cut out a sling as well. Princess Allison Angelica's ankles were exposed in a most shocking manner. Roderick gazed at them admiringly, and this time the tutor swooned.

"Really, Wolfram!" Penny said as she washed and bandaged his skewered arm. "You're a terrible swordsman! Don't you think you ought to try some other line of work?"

"I can't help it!" Wolfram admitted. "I'm naturally left-handed!" The poor boy sounded as if he had just confessed to some terrible sin.

"Then fight with your left hand," Princess Penny suggested.

"I couldn't do that!" a shocked Wolfram cried. "It's base! It's sinister and ignoble and dastardly and several other things I can't even say in front of you!"

"Who says so?" Penny asked.

"Why, all the books, all the sages, all the wise men and all the authorities!"

"Did you ever suppose that all the books, all the sages, all the wise men and all the authorities just might be wrong?"

Wolfram had never been so shocked in all his young life. He stared at this plain, rather mousy-looking young girl, who, nonetheless, bandaged wounds like a surgeon and criticized his style like a coach. Could she be right? Allison Angelica was certainly beautiful, but she was also quite useless at the moment. Whereas this ordinary, squinty-eyed girl. . . .

Wolfram was beginning to fall in love, though he wouldn't recognize it for awhile.

And Princess Penny felt a strange attraction to this ungainly would-be knight. Wolfram was hardly handsome, and unless his fighting skills improved considerably, the first evil knight he faced would have him julienned into long, thin strips in less than a minute. The poor boy needed someone to help him.

But love would have to wait. Wolfram was sent home for his arm to heal, and Princess Penny struggled on with her lessons. Her weaving and spinning were adequate, though she preferred working with leather. She never did learn how to sigh or swoon properly, and she still clumped.

When the day came for evil witches and sorcerers to visit the academy and see whom they would like to menace and endanger with their spells, Princess Allison Angelica received twelve bids and was ultimately claimed by a master sorcerer who offered to imprison her in a silver tower trimmed in gold and encrusted with diamonds, with not one but two fire-breathing dragons to keep watch over her. Princess Penelope Persephone did not even get a second look.

On the following day, it was the turn of graduating princes, knights-to-be, wandering minstrels in disguise and ambitious sons of deserving widows out seeking their fortunes. This time Allison Angelica was bid for by everyone, and was the subject of three duels before settling on a prince whose royal pedigree could be traced back for twenty-three generations.

Princess Penny was ignored again. One not-overly-ambitious son of a semi-deserving widow did give her a second glance before deciding to go questing instead, and a second-class wandering minstrel did compose a rather rude ballad about her squinty eyes and protruding front teeth, but that was it.

Her year was officially closed as a failure, and she was sent home with the suggestion that if she applied herself a bit more, and if her father was willing to pay double tuition the next year, the academy might consider taking her back.

So Princess Penny spent the summer keeping out of her father's sight. She tramped through the fields and pastures, occasionally stepping in cow droppings, stomped a few snakes, baited her own fish hooks and read as many books as she could find.

She also wondered just why she was stuck with being a princess. She certainly didn't seem suited for the role. If only she could have been a varlet instead! She *knew* she could succeed at that!

Meanwhile, trouble was brewing for King Ambrose the Absent-Minded. He had a new highway built through his kingdom, and it included a bridge which spanned the only river in the realm. Being absent-minded, however, the king had forgotten to hold a dedication feast and give presents to appease the local witches and wizards. One of the sorcerers took offense, and sent a troll to haunt the bridge.

Since it was a relatively small bridge over a relatively small river, it received a relatively small troll. However, even small trolls can be very nasty, and this one was particularly so. It slew men, women and children at random, dragging them down to its lair under the river to feed on them, and then strewing their bones about in a most revolting manner.

The required number of complaints and petitions from distraught relatives of the slain having been received, King Ambrose ordered his knights to slay the offending troll and relieve the people of their distress. But this was easier ordered than accomplished.

It is quite easy for a knight in shining armor (or even dull armor, for that matter) to slay a troll, if he can lure it out onto open ground. But what this small but rather nasty troll lacked in size, it more than made up for in cunning.

It refused to be lured from the riverbank and the mud and slime under the bridge. Knights sat on their horses in the meadows by the river and hurled challenges and epithets at it — which is a polite way of saying they called it all sorts of names — but the troll would only tread water and make faces at them. The more they challenged, the more it laughed, and the worse its facial contortions became. A troll is remarkably ugly even when it is *not* making faces.

Most knights gave up in disgust. One lost his temper and charged into the river; but the troll submerged, tripped the horse, and the poor knight fell from the saddle and drowned. The troll made several meals from both knight and horse, and then proceeded to scatter the armor and bones about in a most disgusting and gruesome manner.

115

"An ordinary knight will not suffice," the survivors informed the king. "You must engage the services of a champion."

"Oh dear!" said the king. "Will the Royal Budget permit it?"

"Champions do not fight for money, Sire," the remembrancer informed him. "They will fight only for the hand of a fair princess."

"But do we have one?" asked King Ambrose the Absent-Minded.

"There is your daughter, Sire," the remembrancer again reminded him.

"You mean that plain little creature who makes strange sounds at dinner and wears boots that smell of cow droppings?"

"Sire, she is no longer little," the remembrancer urged.

"But is there a champion who will fight for *her* hand?"

"Advertise, Sire," the remembrancer said. "All things are possible, though some are less likely than others."

So proclamations were printed and distributed to champions and would-be champions far and wide, stating that the hand of Princess Penelope Persephone (and the rest of her as well) would be given in marriage to whomsoever champion would rid King Ambrose's realm of a most troublesome and disgusting troll.

No one responded. The more ambitious champions had their minds set on battles with dragons, giants and evil wizards. The marginal champions, who might have considered taking on a single troll as a way of bolster-

116

ing their reputations, blanched at the idea of winning Princess Penny's hand. Rumors of her year at the academy had also spread far and wide.

"Stronger measures are called for. Sire," the remembrancer said. "I suggest you announce that the princess will be sacrificed to the troll to appease its wrath. . . unless a champion steps forward to fight for her."

"But what if no one does?" the king asked.

"All things are possible, Sire," the remembrancer repeated, "though some are less likely than others. However, there is nothing else we can do." This was not quite true, but the remembrancer was terribly overworked and did not think the princess was good for the kingdom's image anyway.

So a second proclamation was issued, announcing that the Fair Princess Penelope Persephone (an exaggeration, but this was advertising and the king was desperate) would be sacrificed to the troll to appease its wrath. . . unless, of course, a champion would be so kind as to step forward to fight for her life, her honor and her hand. The king and all the court hoped that this would shame the champions into sending one of their number to do battle and save her.

But none of them would.

The troll was elated. It didn't care a fig about looks. To it the princess was a week's worth of dinners, with perhaps a late-night snack or two thrown in. Princesses, no matter what their looks, were supposed to be tender. Its last victims had been a grizzled old mule driver and his grizzled old mule, and the one had been as tough and as tasteless as the other.

Besides, the troll had a reputation to consider. Very few trolls ever got the chance to dine on a princess. A champion always turned up at the last minute, lured the troll onto unfavorable ground and then proceeded to chop it up into small, easily-disposable pieces.

But this troll was too smart for that (or so it thought). It would not be lured, even in the unlikely event that a champion did show up (it was sure that none would). The princess would be sacrificed, its reputation among trolls would skyrocket, and it would *not* be appeased. . . not for long, at any rate!

On the day before the sacrifice, a message was received from one Wolfram, a student-in-training for knighthood, begging the favor of being allowed to fight for the life, favor and hand of Princess Penelope Persephone, if he could be granted the temporary rank of Honorary Champion. (Or it might have been the honorary rank of Temporary Champion. The rules were a bit unclear.)

The king was delighted and happy to comply. To have his only daughter sacrificed without a fight would have been a terrible blow to his prestige. Besides, he had grown quite fond of her over the summer, and did not even mind the smell of her boots or the sounds she occasionally made at supper.

The Royal Bookmakers set the odds at three to one in favor of the troll. But when Wolfram appeared that evening, the odds immediately jumped to six to one, and there were very few takers.

For it was obvious that Wolfram's right arm had not yet healed completely. He no longer wore a sling, but it was still bandaged. His forehand stroke would be weak, and rumor had it that Young Wolfram had no backhand at all. So all the hearts save two in the kingdom were saddened: the troll's, of course, and, strangely enough, Princess Penny's.

She took Wolfram aside for a long, private conversation. Wolfram was seen first to shake his head in denial, then stare in amazement and finally smile in approval. The Royal Bookmakers cut the odds back to three to one, but they still remained in favor of the troll.

The rules of combat in this case were simple. The princess was to be bound to a stake at the water's edge, while troll and champion fought for the right to marry or devour her, as the case might be. To the victor went the spoils, though the princess did not like to think of herself in those terms.

Great was the shock when Wolfram appeared on the field without horse, lance or armor. Indeed, he carried nothing but a sword and buckler, the very weapons he had used in his ill-fated clash with Roderick. The odds on the troll immediately shot back up to six to one.

Nor did Wolfram wear the customary scarf as a token of his lady fair. He wore Princess Penny's boots instead. They did smell faintly of cow droppings, but they also gave him firm and sure footing on the damp grass next to the riverbank.

"Can yonder Wolfram actually prevail in such a manner?" the king wondered.

"All things are possible, Sire," the remembrancer repeated, "though some are much less likely than others."

The troll rose from the waters beneath the bridge and snarled. This was the standard opening move, and it was supposed to goad the champion into some rash action. But Wolfram ignored it.

Instead, he sauntered carelessly over to the stake where the princess was bound. Then the troll waved its long, hairy arms and made faces. This almost always worked, but Wolfram paid no attention. He began to chat with the princess instead. It looked as if they were discussing the weather or the latest court gossip. The troll screamed with rage and actually jumped up and down in the water. This is a very difficult feat, but an angry troll can do it, and this troll was angry indeed! Trolls, you see, have an inferiority complex, being among the least of monsters, and they cannot bear the thought that champions do not respect them.

Princess Penny had discovered this fact in her reading and informed Wolfram of it the night before. Now they reviewed their plan. "Glance at him and yawn." Princess Penny urged. "Try to look bored. We have to make him lose control."

Wolfram felt more terrified than bored, but he glanced at the gibbering troll and managed a fairly realistic yawn. The troll screamed even louder and beat the water with its hands. Wolfram yawned again and then turned his back on it.

The troll lost the rest of its temper and with it all of its cunning and patience too. How dare this third-rate excuse for a champion belittle it! How dare they send a mere boy who wouldn't even arm himself properly! Well, it would show them! It would tear both champion *and* princess to pieces! Then they would have to respect it!

The troll dashed from the river, waving its long, hairy arms and gnashing its terrible teeth. It did not even stop to grab its own weapons. A puny boy like this would be no match! It would tear him apart with its bare hands!

Wolfram raised his sword and tried to look bored, even though his heart was threatening to thump its way right out of his chest. He and the princess had made the plan; now he had to carry it out! As the troll closed in, Wolfram skimmed the buckler at its head. He had, it seems, been holding it instead of wearing it. The troll raised its right arm to ward it off. Its left arm was already extended to wrench the sword from Wolfram's right hand.

But Wolfram flipped his sword from right hand to left, ducked under the extended arm, and ran the sword straight through the troll's wicked heart!

The troll looked hurt, vexed and frustrated all at once. It tried to say, "Left-handed isn't fair!" But it was dead before it could get the words out.

"Gadzooks!" cried the king. "Do mine eyes deceive me? Or did yon Wolfram actually overcome the monster?"

"All things are possible, Sire," said the remembrancer, "and some are more likely than others."

So the highway was saved, the king's reputation was saved, and, most importantly, Princess Penelope Persephone was saved. Wolfram was knighted on the spot and given the title of Sir Wolfram the Trollslayer. He immediately announced his engagement to the princess, and his retirement from active service. For Sir Wolfram was no fool. He knew that, even left-handed, he was at best a mediocre swordsman.

The wedding was a small, quiet affair, though the princess did make sure that all the realm's wizards and sorcerers were invited and appeased. She did *not* want to go through all the trouble and bother of being a sacrifice again! But the wizards and sorcerers were satisfied, and from that day on the kingdom was free from trolls.

Princess Penny and Sir Wolfram moved into the palace, lived there for many years and raised a large family. None of their children were handsome or beautiful, but they were all kind, honest and remarkably intelligent. In fact, many of their descendants are active in the arts and sciences today.

The Bear Hunters

When Michael failed to appear for the fifth straight night, Bunky the Bear knew something was wrong. One night away from the room with the single bunk bed and the cowboy quilt meant a night at some friend's house. Two nights meant a weekend with grandparents. Sometimes in the summer Michael was away at a place called camp for up to seven nights. . . .

But it wasn't summer yet.

Changing position during the day was impossible. In fact, it was prohibited by the Revised International Teddy Bear Code of Conduct. But by night Bunky was free to act. So on the fifth night he moved.

A teddy bear by day is a motionless lump, but by night he or she can become the most agile creature known (or unknown) to man, able to slide from the grasp of a sleeping child without causing the slightest murmur or to slip past the most alert watchdog or prowling cat as if they were mere stone statues.

Bunky crept down the stairs, past the family dog and out onto the porch without any trouble. He shivered for a moment as he realized that he had not been outdoors for weeks, and that his stuffing had grown used to the warmth inside. Then he set off across the lawn for the Randall House.

He found Francis lying on the floor beside his human's bed, a look of worry that only another teddy bear would notice on his face. "What's up? What's down?" Bunky asked in a teddy bear whisper, which is so soft that it makes the drone of a mosquito sound like the roar of a chainsaw.

"I'm worried!" Francis answered in the same tone. "Timmy has been gone for five nights now. It's not like him!"

"Five nights?" Bunky whistled. It sounded like a cricket inside cotton padding. "So has Michael! I don't like this!"

"Do you think they're away at camp together?" Francis asked.

"I think it's too early for camp," Bunky answered. "Maybe Poobah knows something. Let's go ask him."

Francis looked uncomfortable. "I haven't been outside in a long time," he complained.

"It's not a bad night," Bunky reassured him. "Come on! The air will do your stuffing good!"

So the two bears crept outside, across the street and into the house on the corner. Poobah, who had only one ear, did not hear them until they were halfway up the stairs.

"Come in," he called softly. "Jenny's not here."

"That's why we came to see you," Bunky replied as he and Francis settled on the bed. "Michael has been gone for five nights now, and so has Timmy."

"And so has Jenny!" echoed Poobah.

"She shouldn't be with them," Francis observed. "Timmy's at the age where he hates girls." He pointed to a group of dolls on a shelf by the bed. "Do they know anything?" he asked.

"Them?" Poobah snorted. "All they ever notice is their clothes and their hair! You could change humans on them and they'd never know the difference!" He thought for a moment. "But I have heard crying from humans downstairs," he added.

"I think we had all better go see the general," Bunky decided.

General John J. (Black Jack) Panda was a three-generation bear who lived in the attic of the big house next to the park. After helping to bring up the grandson of

125

his original human, he had been retired with full honors. Now he served as a consultant to other teddy bears and spent the rest of his time dictating his memoirs to his secretary, a tattered and faithful Raggedy Ann doll.

The general had a fearsome temper, caused by stuffing that grew steadily lumpier. Because of this, few bears cared to consult him. But General Black Jack Panda knew a great many things. He even knew how to read.

"Well!" he harrumphed as Bunky, Francis and Poobah crept into his attic. "To what do I owe the pleasure of this visit? In other words, what favor do you want this time?"

"We're worried. . ." Bunky began.

"Of course you are!" the general snapped. "Bears never come to see me unless they're worried about something! What is it this time?"

"It's about our children. . ." Francis tried to explain.

"Been mistreating you again, have they? Tchah! You're built to take it! Part of the job! Grit your stitching and keep your powder dry! A little pounding never hurt anyone! Why, I can remember when. . ."

"Not that!" Poobah interrupted. "They've disappeared!"

"Disappeared, y'say? Nonsense!" The general jumped up and began to pace rapidly back and forth, while the tattered and faithful Raggedy Ann kept in step one pace behind him as she took notes. "Children don't disappear; they grow up! Foolish habit, that! They don't know when they're well off!"

"Sir?" Poobah questioned. General Panda's outbursts were sometimes hard for a bear with only one ear to follow.

"Stuffing!" the general continued while Raggedy Ann took notes. "Always shoveling more stuffing into their faces! And those things they call clothes; always changing 'em around! They should pick one size and one covering and stick with it! Why, as I said to old Teddy Ursavelt just before we charged up San Bruin Hill. . ."

"But General!" Bunky quickly interrupted. "Our children really have disappeared! They've all been gone for five days now!"

"And it's the wrong time of year for them to be gone so long!" Francis put in. "They're supposed to be in a place called school, even though Timmy doesn't like it very much."

"And anyway, Jenny never plays with Timmy or Michael. Why should she be gone too? Something has to be wrong!" Poobah concluded.

General John J. Panda was lost in thought. Only a teddy bear would notice the lines of worry on his seemingly placid face, but they were there.

"We cannot act without intelligence," he said at last.

"We've got intelligence!" Poobah objected. "We're not dumb!"

"*Military* intelligence!" General Panda snapped. "Facts! Reports! Secret messages from spies! That's what you can do! Go! Gather intelligence for me!"

"How?" Bunky asked.

The general resumed his pacing. "We can't risk a radio, even up here. Bring me newspapers!"

"What kind?" Francis asked. "We can't read!"

"You bring 'em; I'll read 'em!" Black Jack Panda ordered. "Bring what looks interesting! Now off with you, and report back at 0100 hours!" They stared at him. "One a.m.," he explained.

"We can't tell time either," Bunky admitted.

"As quickly as you can then!" the general harrumphed. "I really don't know what this new crop of bears is coming to!" he grumbled to the tattered and faithful Raggedy Ann as Bunky, Francis and Poobah scurried out of the attic.

Each bear returned with an armload of newspapers, but a teddy bear armload is quite small. "What does this mean?" Bunky asked as he spread a page before the general. "It's got pictures of humans doing strange things."

"Sports page," General Panda informed him. "That's what humans call a baseball game. Hmmm! Let's see how the Cubs are doing." (The general was a great fan of the Chicago Cubs, the Chicago Bears and the Boston Bruins.)

"Uh, General, Sir, hadn't we better get on with it?" Francis asked. "Our children wouldn't be playing with the Cubs, would they?"

"Probably not," Black Jack Panda agreed. "Let's see what Poobah brought. No, these are comics, dealing, from what I can tell, with the adventures of some fat orange cat. No, I need a page with writing on it!" He began to pace again.

"No pictures?" asked a somewhat disappointed Francis.

"No pic. . . Wait! Stop! Yes! Of course!" The general spun around so suddenly that he knocked the tattered and faithful Raggedy Ann over. "Sorry, m'dear," he said as he gallantly helped her up again. "Now, where was I?"

"No pic wait stop yes of course," the doll read from her notes.

"If something has happened to the children," General Panda explained, "then their pictures will be in the paper. Go through the papers for the past five days. They'd be the ones near the top of the stack. If you see pictures of any of your children, then bring me those pages. Now off with you!"

Bunky was the first to return. He had run so hard that his stuffing ached, but he carried a single section of newspaper. Close behind him came Poobah and Francis with copies of the same section. The general spread them out on the floor to examine them.

Each page showed the same pictures of two boys and a girl. Above the pictures were words in big, dark print. "Three Children Kidnapped," the general read aloud. Then he began reading the lines of smaller print silently. There were a great many lines, and the seams on his face began to pucker with worry as he read.

"What does it say?" Bunky asked impatiently.

"What does 'kidnapped' mean?" Francis added.

129

"Is it serious?" Poobah wondered.

Raggedy Ann even stopped taking notes.

"Yes, It's serious!" General Panda said at last. "Kidnappings can be tragic. I knew the Lindbergh Bear once, and he said. . ."

"But what happened to our humans?" Francis insisted.

"Apparently Timmy's mother was taking them all to school," the general explained. "That's why they were all together. Her car was forced off the road by two men who tried to grab Timmy. Timmy's mother and Michael and Jenny all tried to help him. Then Timmy's mother got hit on the head and knocked out. When she came to, all three children were gone."

"But why would someone do that?" Francis asked.

General Panda read on. "It says here," he continued, "the police suspect the two men were hired by Timmy's father. His parents are divorced and Timmy lives with his mother. But nobody knows why they took the other two."

"What can we do then?" Bunky asked.

"We can act!" General Black Jack Panda snapped. "We can find the children and rescue them!"

"How do we do that?" Poobah wondered.

"Military strategy!" Black Jack Panda drew himself up to his full 22 1/2 inches. His voice took on the crisp tone of command. He was once again General John J. Panda, Terror of the Kaiser's Imperial Bears, with a campaign to plan and a staff to direct.

"A new notebook, Miss Ann!" he thundered to his secretary. "Head it: 'Campaign of the Missing Children'. Item One: Objectives. Locate three missing children of the human species and rescue same!" He paused while the tattered and faithful Raggedy Ann scribbled furiously.

"Item Two: Forces at our disposal. One squad of teddy bears, three in number, with no military experience."

"Michael used to play soldiers with me!" Bunky objected.

"*Limited* military experience," the general corrected. "Item Three: Estimation of enemy strength. Two or more adults of the human species, experience and abilities unknown."

General Panda was pacing again, stitches taught with concentration. The tattered and faithful Raggedy Ann kept right in step and scribbled as fast as she could. "Item Four: Location of enemy headquarters."

He stopped short, causing another collision and spilling Raggedy Ann once again. "Francis!" he barked as he helped the doll up. "Did Timmy ever take you to his father's house?"

"Yes, two or three times," Francis answered. "It was an apartment. You don't think the children are there, do you?"

"Of course not!" the general harrumphed. "The human police would have found 'em if they were. But he knows where they are, if anyone does!" He frowned his most ferocious teddy bear frown. "We'll have to make him talk!"

"It's a long way to his apartment," Francis said doubtfully. "We had to go there in a car."

"How long did it take?" the general asked.

Francis thought as hard as he could, but minutes and hours meant very little to a teddy bear. "Part of a day," he finally said. "We left after Timmy put in his morning stuffing, and we got there before he got his midday stuffing."

"Hmmm!" the general frowned. "Perhaps an hour or two then. Did the car go very fast?"

"Any car seems fast to me," Francis said.

"Did it start up and slow down a lot?" the general asked.

Francis brightened. "Yes, I remember that! Timmy's mother said something about hitting all the reds, but I didn't think she hit anything."

"Very good!" said General Panda. "That means he probably lives somewhere in this city, perhaps over on the other side. Very well. Item five: Transport. We must all get over there."

"How?" Poobah asked.

"It's way too far to run, and I don't even know the way," Francis added doubtfully.

"Then we must find someone who does," the general replied. "The obvious answer is Timmy's mother." He frowned again. "Now listen carefully! Here's what we all must do. . . ."

Ten minutes later Francis was back in his house, had dodged the family cat and made his way back up the stairs to where Timmy's mother lay sleeping. He paused and went over the general's instructions. Whisper so softly that she hears without waking, but keep repeating the message until she understands.

Francis had never talked to a grownup before. He had held conversations with a sleeping Timmy; what bear hasn't talked to a sleeping child when it wants a headlock relaxed or unconscious ear-chewing stopped? Well, grownups were supposed to be just large children. He took a teddy bear version of a deep breath and began to whisper.

"Timmy needs his teddy bear!" He repeated it several times. "Take the teddy bear to his father!" Again he repeated the message. "His father will get the bear to him. Wake up and get the bear! Do it now! Do it now!" He slid off the bed and waited to see what would happen.

Timmy's mother tossed and turned. Then Francis saw an eyelid flicker. He quickly scooted to Timmy's room, and when Timmy's mother got there a few minutes later, Francis was lying on the bed with a face as blank as a grownup thinks a teddy bear's face should be, must be, and always is.

Timmy's mother picked him up, hugged him once and made for the garage, all the while muttering to herself, "This is crazy!"

She opened the driver's door and leaned over to put him on the passenger seat. It took her just two seconds to set him down, but in those two seconds, three small shapes slipped from the shadows and into the back of the car. The rescue campaign had begun!

According to the general, the trip took only twenty minutes. But traffic was light at two in the morning. The car pulled up suddenly before a row of apartments. Timmy's mother rang the bell on one of the doors. She had to ring several times before a man finally answered. He did not look happy.

"I. . . I brought this for Timmy," she explained as she handed Francis over to the startled, sleepy man. "It's his teddy bear, remember? He needs it."

"I've told you, and I've told the cops," the man answered with a sleepy groan. "I don't know where Timmy or the others are! I'm just as baffled and worried as you are!" To a human it might have sounded convincing, but Francis could feel the lie in his voice.

"But he may show up here, and he needs it," Timmy's mother insisted.

"Couldn't it wait until morning?" the man grumbled.

"I had a dream," she tried to explain. "It all seemed so real. A voice was telling me that Timmy needed his bear right away, and you would know how to get it to him." She began to cry and then turned away. "Sorry if I woke you," she said and got back in her car and drove off.

But while the two humans talked, the other three bears had slipped from the car and into the apartment.

Timmy's father shrugged, tossed Francis on a couch and went back to bed. Francis waited until he was asleep again before calling the others.

"Terrible housekeeper!" the general complained as he squirmed out from behind the couch. "Place hasn't been properly cleaned in weeks; never would have passed muster in my day!"

"When do we start?" Francis asked.

"Immediately!" General Panda snapped. "We don't have much time before morning!"

Nothing in the world is as gentle and yet at the same time as ruthlessly thorough as a teddy bear questioning session. Francis snuggled under the sleeping man's arm. Poobah settled close to one ear and began humming lullabies in a voice three times lower than a spring breeze. Bunky stationed himself at the other ear, ready to ask the questions. General Panda sat watching gravely. Then he nodded.

"What is your name?" Bunky asked in a voice as soft as falling tissue paper.

"Paul Randall," came the muttered response. The arm squeezed Francis closer. The worry lines on the man's face relaxed.

"Are you Timmy's father?"

"Yes."

"Do you know what happened to him and the others?" Bunky fought to keep his voice calm. This was the big one.

"Roy 'n Earl. . . all a mistake," the man mumbled.

"What happened?" Bunky asked.

"Wanted Timmy. . . go away with him. . . another town, another state. . . have him for myself. . ." He talked in spurts between long, deep breaths. The bears tried to understand.

"Not fair. . . only see him now and then. . . take him where she'll never find. . ."

Bunky suddenly understood. This was a great big child, spoiled and selfish. He wanted it all and never wanted to share. Humans were supposed to grow out of that, but apparently some never did.

"Roy 'n Earl. . . said they'd get him. . . grab him. . . way to school. . . didn't know. . . car pool. . . others fought. . . panicked. . . took all three kids. . . Don't know what to do now. . ."

"Are they safe?" Bunky asked.

"Roy 'n Earl got 'em. . . figure out a way. . . get the others back. . . don't want to hurt. . ."

"Where are they?" Bunky broke in. General Panda frowned, then nodded. Interrupting was dangerous, but the night would not last much longer, and they might still have a long way to go.

"Old fishing cabin. . . hour from here. . . belongs to Roy. . . wait. . . get 'em back. . . after heat dies down. . ."

"Do you know the way?"

"Been there twice. . . kids asleep. . . nobody saw me. . . took food. . ."

Bunky looked at General Panda, who nodded again. They had the information. Now it was time to act!

"Timmy needs his teddy bear," Bunky told the sleeping man. "Take it there tonight. Take the bear tonight! Take the bear tonight!" He repeated his whispered command until the man began to stir. Then the four bears quietly left the room.

When Timmy's father came out a few minutes later, Francis was back on the couch and the others were hidden. The man took Francis out to the car and tossed him on the front seat. Then he got behind the wheel and yawned once before slamming the door. During that three-second yawn, he got three extra passengers.

It was an exciting trip. Timmy's father drove very fast for someone who was so sleepy. The general, who had flown with Captain Eddie Rickenbruin, took it all quite calmly. But the stuffings were rumbling in the other three bears, and they were glad when he stopped for some coffee at an all-night cafe.

Soon after the coffee stop, they left the city and the bright lights behind. Timmy's father kept turning onto different roads, and each seemed narrower, windier and bumpier than the one before. Finally the car slowed and then stopped.

Timmy's father blinked the lights three times and then got out. He took Francis with him, but the other three bears were also out and hiding under the car before he could close the door again.

They followed him up a path to an old shack. Francis could see a light behind one of the windows. A door opened and two men came out. One was thin and the other was fat. Why do humans never seem to have the right amount of stuffing? Francis wondered.

"Any news?" the fat one asked. Francis couldn't make out his face, but the voice sounded worried.

"Are they all asleep?" Timmy's father asked in turn.

"Yeah," said the thin man. He did not sound happy either.

"I brought Timmy's bear. See that he gets it, Okay?"

"You came all the way out here in the dead of night just to deliver a teddy bear?" the fat man asked in amazement.

Timmy's father blinked. It had been a strange night for him, and the realization of what he had done was just beginning to sink in. "Yeah, don't know why I did it," he said.

"You sure nobody followed you?" the thin man asked.

Timmy's father nodded, even though he wasn't sure. It had all been like a dream. He thought he remembered voices. . . .

"Okay," the thin man said. "But you've got just one more day to figure a way outa this, 'cause we ain't watchin' these kids here any longer! One more day, then either you take 'em or we leave 'em! You got that?"

The two men walked back to the shack with Francis as Timmy's father got in his car and drove off. He didn't even come in to look at him, Francis thought. He only cares about himself.

Bunky, Poobah and the general were already hidden inside.

The three children lay on makeshift cots. They were asleep, but Francis and the others could tell that it was a troubled sleep and full of bad dreams. The thin man looked at his watch.

"Almost four o'clock, Roy," he said. "I'm not gonna get back to sleep. You watch 'em and I'll go to an all-nighter for some coffee and grub."

"You went last time!" Roy protested.

"They don't like seeing my face when they first wake up," said Earl. "You keep watch. I'll be back in an hour."

He left and Roy settled back in a big chair and closed his eyes. Francis, Bunky and Poobah quickly joined their humans. The children did not wake up, but their sleep became easier and the bad dreams went away. The general waited until Roy was asleep and then crawled up in the big man's lap.

When Earl came back an hour later, he found all three children cuddling teddy bears. And Roy was sound asleep in his chair, snuggling a fourth bear and sucking his thumb. His face was as happy and peaceful as the children's.

"Roy! Wake up! Where'd all them bears come from?" Earl whispered as he shook the fat man awake.

"Aw, Earl! Why'd ya hafta wake me up? I was having the bestest dream!"

"Never mind the dream! Where'd ya get that bear?"

Roy, suddenly wide awake, stared down at the now-blank face of General Black Jack Panda. "Why, I don't rightly know! Last thing I remember was. . . Hey! All three of them kids got bears now! And where'd this here one come from? What's goin' on here, Earl?"

"That's what *I'm* askin' *you!*" Earl replied. "You mean to say nobody came in while I was gone?"

"Naw, Earl! I'd a'known if they had!"

"But one bear's done turned into four!" Earl began to shake. "I don't like this, Roy! I'm afraid that if I sit down and close my eyes, I'll wake up in a whole room fulla bears!"

"What do you reckon we do then?" Roy asked.

"I never liked this idea, even before them multiplyin' bears come along!" Earl said. "Let's get outa here now!"

"But we can't leave them kids alone!" Roy protested.

"We'll call the cops from a pay phone," Earl said as he picked up two dirty rags. "Help me wipe this place clean of prints, and we'll be miles down the road a'fore anyone wakes up!"

"Can I take this here bear with me?" Roy asked.

"No! No bears and no kids, never again!"

The police arrived an hour later. They found three children sleeping with their teddy bears, and General Panda keeping watch. Roy and Earl were never seen again.

Nor was Timmy's father. Roy and Earl must have tipped him off, because he vanished too. Timmy was sad for a while, and Francis shared his sorrow, because that is part of a teddy bear's duty.

The general told him that the hurt would grow dimmer, but a part of it would always remain.

"Humans have these things called feelings, and they are hurt very easily," he explained. "That is why they need us so much."

The children got into a big argument over who would get to keep the general. They finally agreed to share him, but then they got into another argument over who would get to have him first and for how long. The general finally put an end to it by getting himself lost. He fled back to the attic in the old house by the park. There he went back to his old job of teddy bear consultant, that is, except for when he was dictating an account of his great adventures to the tattered and faithful Raggedy Ann.

The Fox and the Squirrel
(a fable with two endings and one moral)

A fox once sat under a tree in a meadow and wept bitterly. "Alas!" it cried. "Such a sorrowful fate is mine!"

"Why do you weep?" asked a squirrel who perched on a branch above it. "The day is warm, the sun is bright, the air is pure and life seems good. And yet you cry in the midst of beauty."

"I weep because of my sad fate," the fox replied. "Tonight I must sneak like the thief that I am down into the farmer's hencoop and steal one of his chickens."

"That's a sad fate for the chicken, but why for you?" asked the squirrel. "A fox must eat, after all. All creatures must. That is why I gather nuts."

"I don't see you down here gathering them right now," observed the fox.

"Fate says a fox must eat, but fate does not say a squirrel has to be the meal, not if the squirrel chooses to be careful."

"Meaning that you don't trust me?" asked the fox.

"Exactly!" the squirrel agreed.

"Alas! That is my sad fate!" cried the fox. "Nobody will be my friend. No one will share my joys and sorrows. I am an outcast, and everyone's hand is against me. Do you know what will happen when I raid that hencoop tonight?"

"I have a fairly good idea," said the squirrel.

"All the chickens will squawk and carry on like the end of the world is at hand — *all* of them, mind you — not just the one I take. I wouldn't blame it for complaining, but what concern is it to the others? I'm not harming them, am I? Then the farmer will come out with his dogs and his gun, and I will have to run for my life. They will do their best to hunt me down and destroy me. And why?"

"Do you really want me to answer that?" said the squirrel.

"You don't have to," said the fox. "I know it is because I am a fox, and that is what my nature compels me to do. Must I always be blamed for what nature compels me to do? Now, suppose I became a squirrel like you."

"You would look very odd sitting up here," the squirrel observed, "and I don't think a diet of nuts and seeds would do you much good."

"But you are loved!" argued the fox. "You can sit in the farmer's orchard in the middle of the day and eat from his trees, and he thinks nothing of it! He even puts food out for you in the winter! Do you think he would ever set out a chicken for me when the snows are deep?"

"I doubt it very much," said the squirrel.

"Of course not!" the fox agreed. "He will try to kill me on sight, even if I have never gone near his precious hencoop! I am branded a killer and an outlaw with never a chance to clear my reputation or speak in my own defense!"

"Life can be hard," said the squirrel. "I feel sorry for you, but I'm still going to stay up here out of reach."

"Your sorrow does me no good," said the fox. "Would you consider helping me tonight, though?"

"If it does not mean leaving the safety of this tree, I might think about it," said the squirrel.

Again the fox began to weep. "How sad it is never to be trusted!" it complained bitterly. "Still, I must make the most of your kind offer, even though you make it most unkindly."

"Just tell me what you want," the squirrel said.

"Simply this," the fox replied. "Tonight, when I journey to the hencoop, I will come across the meadow from the left and pass right under your tree. On the way back, with the chicken, I will run straight to the tree and then veer off to the right. As soon as I do, you come down from the tree and brush out my tracks with your long, beautiful and extremely useful bushy tail."

"And wind up as the second course for your dinner?" the squirrel asked mockingly.

"How can I grab you when my mouth is already full of chicken?" the fox argued reasonably. "Besides, you don't have to erase them all the way across the meadow. Just do it far enough so that the dogs will follow the wrong track off to the left."

"*If* I do this, what will you do for me?" the squirrel asked.

"Tomorrow I will gather the finest nuts I can find on the forest floor and bring them right to the base of your tree," said the fox.

It held up a paw to forestall the squirrel's objection. "*And* I will retreat all the way to the forest before you come down, because I know you do not trust me." It shed another tear at the injustice of it all.

The squirrel considered the offer and then nodded. "Very well," it said. "I will cover your retreat, *if* I see you with a chicken in your mouth. But will you keep your end of the bargain?"

"Of course, I will!" said the fox in a slightly offended voice. "For if this works, it could mean a great profit for both of us."

"It could also lessen the danger to both of us," the squirrel agreed. "Very well, we will try it tonight!"

So that night the fox crept down from the forest, across the meadow past the squirrel's tree and made its way down to the farmyard. Not long after the squirrel heard a tremendous outcry from the hencoop and saw the fox running back across the meadow with a chicken in its mouth. When it reached the tree, the fox veered off in the opposite direction from that in which it had come.

The squirrel waited only until the fox was out of sight, then it scampered down the tree and began rubbing out the fox's fresh tracks with its long, bushy tail, and at the same time covering the fox's scent with its own. When it heard the dogs coming in pursuit, it raced back up the tree to watch.

The dogs charged straight across the meadow to the squirrel's tree, hesitated for a moment, then ran off in the wrong direction, following the fox's old track. Close behind them came the farmer with his gun.

Well, that part worked, the squirrel said to itself. Now, will the fox keep its end of the deal or have I made a bad bargain? But the next morning the fox appeared with a mouthful of nuts which it spat out at the base of the squirrel's tree. "I don't see how you can stand to eat such stuff!" it complained.

"And I don't see how you can stand to eat raw meat," the squirrel answered. "I might also add that one mouthful of nuts is not a very great reward for the risks I took last night."

"I can only bring one mouthful at a time," the fox protested. "But you shall have more!" And back to the forest it went and returned with another mouthful. It had to make three trips before the squirrel was satisfied.

"You drive a hard bargain," the fox protested.

"And you are alive and well with a full stomach," said the squirrel. "Don't complain so much."

"Very well," the fox agreed. "Tonight the farmer will guard the hencoop closely, so I will keep clear. But in two or three days he will relax and I will go back. Then we can try our scheme once more, if you are willing to work with me again."

"Oh, I am willing enough," said the squirrel. "But this time I want to be paid in advance."

"You are becoming a greedy rogue," the fox complained.

"I'm sure it is due to the company I keep," said the squirrel.

So the squirrel and the fox worked together once more, and again the partnership was a success. The squirrel got another supply of nuts, and the fox escaped with another chicken.

FIRST ENDING

One day the fox thought: the squirrel is getting fatter than I am from this bargain. I must bring it a supply of nuts every day, but it only covers my tracks twice a week. That is hardly fair. Besides, the supply of chickens is decreasing, and it is getting more and more difficult to break into the hencoop. Perhaps it is time to dissolve the partnership.

So, on its next raid, the fox ran only as far as the edge of the forest. There it dropped the chicken it carried and lay in wait for the squirrel. When it had brushed its way far enough from the tree, the fox dashed out, seized it, and so had a choice of dinners that night. For it had seen how the squirrel had grown fat and lazy from its easy living.

SECOND ENDING

One day the squirrel thought: I am taking a huge risk to benefit a rogue. The dogs might catch me on the ground or the farmer may well discover what I am doing. Then I will be killed instead of the fox. Perhaps it is time to dissolve the partnership.

So, on the fox's next raid, the squirrel erased its first set of tracks. Then, when the fox ran back with the chicken, the squirrel stayed where it was and watched the dogs follow the fox to its hiding place at the edge of the forest, where they fell on it and killed it. For the fox had grown lazy and overconfident due to the aid the squirrel had given it.

MORAL

A partnership between two rogues can only end badly, either way.

Kalil the Blind & Brave

In a kingdom that no longer exists and in a time so long ago that no one can any longer remember, there lived a brave warrior named Kalil, who had fought in many battles for his sultan. In one last battle, during the storming of a castle, Kalil was struck in the face by burning oil and therefore blinded and disfigured.

After the battle, Kalil's sword was taken from him, and he was sent home to his village to live out his days in peace and honor.

The folk of Kalil's village, however, were a cruel and selfish people. They had been jealous of Kalil's glory, and now that he was helpless — or so they thought — they refused to honor him. Instead, they forced him to live as a beggar on the streets.

Now it happened that each year, every city and every village in the kingdom had to pay its annual tax and tribute to the sultan. The people of Kalil's village hated this, not only because of their selfishness, but also because the road to the capital was very long and very dangerous. Oftentimes the messenger bringing the taxes would be robbed, or even killed, by the many bandits who lurked along the way.

This one year, the headman of Kalil's village had an idea. "We will load the tax bags with coins of copper, instead of coins of gold," he said, "and we will send them with Kalil the beggar, for he will certainly be robbed and killed along the way! Thus, for a loss of a trifling sum, we will be excused our taxes for a year and be rid of a worthless blind beggar, whom we now must support!"

The other villagers thought this was a fine idea. So the tax bags were loaded with old, worn copper coins, and Kalil the beggar was summoned from his hut.

"You shall take our taxes to the sultan this year," they told him. "Guard them well, lest the bandits rob and slay thee along the way!" And to help him on his journey they gave him a mule, the oldest and lamest one in the village.

Kalil did not mind this. Indeed, he was almost happy, for life in the village had become a torture to him. Truly, he thought, a meeting with a bandit would not be such a bad thing for me. For a bandit is at least honest in his intentions, and does not clothe foul deeds with fair words. If only they had given me a weapon, that I might die fighting! But perhaps Allah may grant me one!

And so Kalil mounted the mule and began his journey.

The first day passed without incident, save that Kalil's old mule was so slow that he was unable to reach the inn where he planned to stay that night. He was forced to camp out in the open which, in truth, saved his life. For a villager more wicked than the others had sent word of Kalil's journey to a powerful bandit named Joram the Terrible, who now lay in wait close by the inn to rob and slay the blind messenger.

As the bandit waited by the inn, Kalil slept out in a meadow under a tree, wrapped in his cloak, and with his saddlebags beneath his head for a pillow.

In the morning, Kalil awoke and felt about him for his whip, for he knew he must force the old mule to a faster pace that day. In his blindness, though, Kalil laid his hand instead upon a deadly snake which had crept beneath his cloak for warmth during the night!

Kalil would have died, then and there, had it not been for the fact that the snake was so numb with the cold that it was unable to strike! In his blindness, Kalil coiled it, and — still believing it to be his whip — placed it in his saddlebags and so resumed his journey.

He had scarcely traveled a mile before he met with Joram the Terrible, who was still seeking him. "Ho, Blind Beggar!" cried the robber. "Commend thy soul to Allah, for I shall certainly leave thy bones for the crows to pick clean along the roadside!"

Thus may jackals taunt a blinded lion, Kalil thought bitterly. If only I had a weapon! And it was then that Kalil thought of his whip!

Well, at least I shall strike a blow, he decided. Perhaps Allah will guide my hand so that I may leave a mark upon him, so that others may know that Kalil died fighting with weapon in hand.

But Allah guided Kalil's hand even more surely than that, for he reached into the saddlebags and grasped the snake by the tail! As the bandit mocked him, Kalil drew what he thought was his whip from the saddlebags and, spurring the old mule forward, struck out at the sound of the robber's voice!

Joram, taken off his guard, could not raise his sword in time to parry the blow. The snake struck him, full on the neck, and the enraged reptile buried its deadly fangs in the robber's throat!

Joram gave a horrible cry and fell dead from his horse, and it was then that Kalil realized: this had been no ordinary whip! He quickly reached forward and grasped the snake behind its head, before it could strike again. He was about to kill it, but then thought better.

"No, Little Brother!" he said to it. "I believe Allah sent thee to save my life and to gain for me a fine horse and a sword. I will return thee to the saddlebags, for thou may be useful once again. Do not, however, think that I will reach for thee so carelessly a second time!"

Kalil next felt around until he found the bandit's sword, cut off Joram's head with it, and placed the head in the robber's saddlebags. Then he transferred his own burden to the robber's horse and turned the old mule loose.

"Take thy rest, my friend!" he called out to it. "For I now have a fine horse and a sword to help me on my way!"

Kalil had been a fine horseman in his day and, blind or not, he still knew how to ride. He gave the bandit's horse free rein and it carried him many miles that day. At nightfall it brought him to the door of yet another inn.

Now the keeper of this inn was a wicked man, who often robbed and murdered lone travelers in their sleep. Usually he drugged their food first, though he did not think that step necessary with a blind traveler like Kalil.

I shall simply wait until he sleeps, the innkeeper thought. Then I shall cut his throat in the middle of the night and take what he has! So, in the dead of night, the wicked innkeeper crept into Kalil's room with a knife, bent on robbery. . . and murder!

"Hmm!" the innkeeper said softly to himself. "Before I cut his throat, I'd best see if he has anything worth taking. For 'tis bothersome to kill a man for nothing!"

Thus, in the darkness, the wicked innkeeper plunged his hand into the saddlebags. The snake struck for the second time!

The innkeeper's screams awoke Kalil and, after the screams had stopped, he felt around until he found the innkeeper's knife, and soon added his head to that of the bandit's! Then he made certain that the snake was secure.

"That's twice thou hast saved my life, Little Brother!" he told it. "This time I shall get thee a piece of the finest cheese that this dog of an innkeeper possesses!"

Since day and night were one to Kalil, he arose and began his search immediately, for there were no other guests at the inn. He found the cheese hidden away in the innkeeper's larder and close beside it, a bag of gold, the proceeds of other robberies!

"Aha!" said Kalil as he hefted the bag. "I fear that others may have come to grief here, but no longer!"

Thus Kalil once more resumed his journey.

Kalil had a safe passage to the capital after that. Many bandits watched him from afar, but none dared close in to attack. "He rides the horse and carries the sword of Joram the Terrible!" they said one to another. "He must be a great warrior indeed! We shall seek our victims elsewhere!"

So, after many days, Kalil arrived at the capital. And, after asking the way, he was given directions to the sultan's palace.

Now it happened that the sultan's grand vizier was returning from a journey of his own, and he and Kalil were shown through the gate and into the palace courtyard together. As they waited for the sultan to receive them, they fell to talking. Thus, the grand vizier learned of Kalil's journey, and of the fact that he was blind.

Now this grand vizier was a cunning, crafty man, who saw in Kalil's journey and in his blindness, a way to win favor for himself in the eyes of the sultan, for in truth, his own journey had been a failure.

He said to Kalil, "Ah, my friend! Thou shouldst know that one does not simply walk in to His Majesty's presence. No indeed! Someone must go before thee to, ah, announce thee and, er, make preparations for His Majesty to receive thee! Know thou also, it is a great wrong to carry a weapon into His Majesty's presence! Therefore I pray thee, give me the sword thou hast taken from the bandit, and I will keep it safe for thee. And take thy horse to the stable for refreshment while I go, ah, make preparations for His Majesty to receive thee!"

Now to this Kalil agreed, although he felt suspicious.

His instincts were correct, for no sooner did Kalil depart with the horse, than the grand vizier rushed into the throne room and cried out, "Your Majesty! I have traveled far through many lands to gather taxes for thee, and have brought thee bags of gold from a village whose taxes have heretofore been stolen by bandits! During my travels, I fell in with a great robber named Joram the Terrible, and slew him after a terrific struggle! In proof of this, I offer you his sword!"

"But where are the rest of his trappings?" asked the sultan.

"Oh, a certain blind beggar, whom I met along the way and on whom I took pity, is stabling the bandit's horse for me. But here, oh Sultan, are the taxes from the village!" And with that, he handed the saddlebags over to the sultan!

However, the sultan was a wise and cautious ruler, and he did not blindly plunge his hand into them. Instead, he opened the bags and emptied their contents onto the floor! And out there fell. . . old, worn copper coins, the cheapest in the land, and a deadly snake!

The sultan was filled with wrath at this act of treachery and cried out, "So! This is the love that you bear for your ruler, is it? Guards! Deal with him!"

The guards fell upon the terrified grand vizier, and cut him into forty pieces then and there, for the sultan believed in swift and severe justice!

"Now bring that blind beggar before me, that I may learn the true meaning of this!" the sultan commanded. So Kalil was brought before the sultan, where he told the story of his journey and why the snake had come with him.

"As to the coins," Kalil said, "I did not know their value, but I believe the villagers meant for them to be stolen. Here, O Sultan, is another bag, which I took from an innkeeper who also tried to murder me. His head, along with Joram's, is in the other saddlebag." And when the sultan opened this bag, a shower of good gold coins fell out!

"Hmm!" said the sultan. "But how came it my late grand vizier did not get his hands on these?"

"Your Majesty, I have lost my sight, but not my wits!" Kalil replied. "I did not trust your grand vizier, so I did not tell him of my suspicions, or of the snake!"

At this the sultan grew stern and said, "And did you not fear that I too might have perished by the snake?"

"No, Your Majesty," Kalil replied. "For I believe that snake was sent by Allah to punish evildoers! Twice he has struck to save my life, and he has proved the guilt of a false advisor. Therefore I pray you, do not kill the snake. Rather, have him taken back to the meadow and released, for he has served us both well!"

"It shall be done," the sultan agreed. "But stay! Are you not Kalil, the great warrior who was blinded in my service and sent to live in peace and honor? Why do you come to me thus dressed as a beggar?"

So it was Kalil told the story of his life in the village, and the sultan said, "My friend, thou hast brought me something far more valuable than gold! Thou hast brought me a brave and trusted servant, thyself, who shall from henceforth live in my palace and be my new grand vizier!"

And the sultan gave orders that Kalil's village be destroyed, and that all its inhabitants be sold as slaves, for he was a stern ruler and harsh in his justice.

Kalil was brought to the palace, where he lived to the end of his days; and they were many indeed!

The End